DIARY of a Wimpy Kid

小屁孩日记⑭

—— 少年格雷的烦恼

［美］杰夫·金尼 著

朱力安 译

老爸的弟弟
——盖瑞叔叔

格雷

·广州·
广东省出版集团
新世纪出版社

本书简体中文版由美国Harry N. Abrams公司通过中国Creative Excellence Rights Agency独家授权

版权合同登记号：19-2013-033号

图书在版编目（CIP）数据

小屁孩日记⑭：少年格雷的烦恼 /（美）杰夫·金尼著；朱力安译. —广州：新世纪出版社，2013.6（2016.6重印）

ISBN 978-7-5405-8118-3/01

Ⅰ.小…　Ⅱ.①杰…　②朱…　Ⅲ.①漫画—作品集—美国—现代　Ⅳ.①J238.2

中国版本图书馆CIP数据核字（2013）第065734号

出 版 人：孙泽军

选题策划：林　铨　王小斌

责任编辑：王小斌　廖晓威　游少波

责任技编：王建慧

小屁孩日记⑭ ——少年格雷的烦恼

XIAOPIHAI RIJI⑭ ——SHAONIAN GELEI DE FANNAO

［美］杰夫·金尼 著　朱力安 译

出版发行：新世纪出版社

　　　　　（广州市大沙头四马路10号　邮政编码：510102）

经　　销：全国新华书店

印　　刷：广东省教育厅教育印刷厂

开　　本：890mm×1240mm　1/32

印　　张：7.25　字　数：120千字

版　　次：2013年6月第1版

印　　次：2016年6月第5次印刷

定　　价：18.50元

质量监督电话：020-83797655　购书咨询电话：020-83781545

"小屁孩之父"杰夫·金尼致中国粉丝

中国的"哈屁族":

你们好!

从小我就对中国很着迷,现在能给中国读者写信真是我的荣幸啊。我从来没想过自己会成为作家,更没想到我的作品会流传到你们的国家,一个离我家十万八千里的地方。

当我还是个小屁孩的时候,我和我的朋友曾试着挖地洞,希望一直挖下去就能到地球另一端的中国。不一会儿,我们就放弃了这个想法(要知道,挖洞是件多辛苦的事儿啊!);但现在通过我的这些作品,我终于到中国来了——只是通过另一种方式,跟我的想象有点不一样的方式。

谢谢你们让《小屁孩日记》在中国成为畅销书。我希望你们觉得这些故事是有趣的,也希望这些故事对你们是一种激励,让你们有朝一日也成为作家和漫画家。我是幸运的,因为我的梦想就是成为一个漫画家,而现在这个梦想实现了。不管你们的梦想是什么,我都希望你们梦想成真。

我希望有朝一日能亲身到中国看看。这是个将要实现的梦想!

希望你们喜欢《小屁孩日记》。再次感谢你们对这套书的喜爱!

 杰夫

A Letter to Chinese Readers

Hello to all my fans in China!

I've had a fascination with China ever since I was a boy, and it's a real privilege to be writing to you now. I never could have imagined that I would become an author, and that my work would reach a place as far from my home as your own country.

When I was a kid, my friends and I tried to dig a hole in the ground, because we hoped we could reach China on the other side of the earth. We gave up after a few minutes (digging is hard!), but with these books, I'm getting to reach your country... just in a different way than I had imagined.

Thank you so much for making **Diary of a Wimpy Kid** a success in your country. I hope you find the stories funny and that they inspire you to become writers and cartoonists. I feel very fortunate to have achieved my dream to become a cartoonist, and I hope you achieve your dream, too... whatever it might be.

I hope to one day visit China. It would be a dream come true!

I hope you enjoy the **Wimpy Kid** books. Thank you again for embracing my books!

Jeff

有趣的书，好玩的书

夏致

  这是一个美国中学男生的日记。他为自己的瘦小个子而苦恼，老是会担心被同班的大块头欺负，会感慨"为什么分班不是按个头分而是按年龄分"。这是他心里一道小小的自卑，可是另一方面呢，他又为自己的脑瓜比别人灵光而沾沾自喜，心里嘲笑同班同学是笨蛋，老想投机取巧偷懒。

  他在老妈的要求下写日记，幻想着自己成名后拿日记本应付蜂拥而至的记者；他特意在分班时装得不会念书，好让自己被分进基础班，打的主意是"尽可能降低别人对你的期望值，这样即使最后你可能几乎什么都不用干，也总能给他们带来惊喜"；他喜欢玩电子游戏，可是他爸爸常常把他赶出家去，好让他多活动一下。结果他跑到朋友家里去继续打游戏，然后在回家的路上用别人家的喷水器弄湿身子，扮成一身大汗的样子；他眼红自己的好朋友手受伤以后得到女生的百般呵护，就故意用绷带把自己的手掌缠得严严实实的装伤员，没招来女生的关注反惹来自己不想搭理的人；不过，一山还有一山高，格雷再聪明，在家里还是敌不过哥哥罗德里克，还是被耍得团团转；而正在上幼儿园的弟弟曼尼可以"恃小卖小"，无论怎么捣蛋都有爸妈护着，让格雷无可奈何。

  这个狡黠、机趣、自恋、胆小、爱出风头、喜欢懒散的男孩，一点都不符合人们心目中的那种懂事上进的好孩子形象，奇怪的是这个缺点不少的男孩子让我忍不住喜欢他。

  人们总想对生活中的一切事情贴上个"好"或"坏"的标签。要是找不出它的实在可见的好处，它就一定是"坏"，是没有价值的。

单纯的有趣，让我们增添几分好感和热爱，这难道不是比读书学习考试重要得多的事情吗？！生活就像一个蜜糖罐子，我们是趴在桌子边踮高脚尖伸出手，眼巴巴地瞅着罐子的孩子。有趣不就是蜂蜜的滋味吗？

翻开这本书后，我每次笑声与下一次笑声之间停顿不超过5分钟。一是因为格雷满脑子的鬼主意和诡辩，实在让人忍俊不禁。二是因为我还能毫不费劲地明白他的想法，一下子就捕捉到格雷的逻辑好笑在哪里，然后会心一笑。

小学二年级的时候我和同班的男生打架；初一的时候放学后我在黑板上写"某某某（男生）是个大笨蛋"；初二的时候，同桌的男生起立回答老师提问，我偷偷移开他的椅子，让他的屁股结结实实地亲吻了地面……我对初中男生的记忆少得可怜，到了高中，进了一所重点中学，大多数的男生要么是专心学习的乖男孩，要么是个性飞扬的早熟少年。除了愚人节和邻班的同学集体调换教室糊弄老师以外，男生们很少再玩恶作剧了。仿佛大家不约而同都知道，自己已经过了有资格耍小聪明，并且耍完以后别人会觉得自己可爱的年龄了。

如果你是一位超过中学年龄的大朋友，欢迎你和我在阅读时光中做一次短暂的童年之旅；如果你是格雷的同龄人，我真羡慕你们，因为你们读了这本日记之后，还可以在自己的周围发现比格雷的经历更妙趣横生的小故事，让阅读的美好体验延续到生活里。

要是给我一个机会再过一次童年，我一定会睁大自己还没有患上近视的眼睛，仔细发掘身边有趣的小事情，拿起笔记录下来。亲爱的读者，不知道当你读完这本小书后，是否也有同样的感觉？

片刻之后我转念一想，也许从现在开始，还来得及呢。作者创作这本图画日记那年是30岁，那么说来我还有9年时间呢。

一种简单的快乐

刘恺威

　　我接触《小屁孩日记》的时间其实并不长，是大约在一年多以前，我从香港飞回横店时，在机场的书店里看到了《小屁孩日记》的漫画。可能每一个人喜爱的漫画风格都不太一样，比如有人喜欢美式的、日系的、中国风的，有人注重写实感的，而我个人就比较偏向于这种线条简单的、随性的漫画，而且人物表情也都非常可爱。所以当时一下子就被封面吸引住了，再翻了翻内容，越看越觉得开心有趣，所以立刻就买下了它。

　　说实话，我并不认为《小屁孩日记》只是一本简单的儿童读物。我向别人推荐它的时候也会说，它是一本可以给大人看的漫画书，可以让整个人都感受到那种纯粹的开心。可能大家或多或少都会有这样的感受，当我们离开学校出来工作以后，渐渐地变得忙碌、和家人聚在一起的时间越来越少，也无法避免地接收到一些压力和负面情绪，对生活和社会的认知也变得更加复杂，有时候会感觉很累，心情烦躁，但如果真的自问为什么会这么累，究竟在辛苦追求着什么的时候，自己却又没有真正的答案……这并不是说我对成年后的生活有多么悲观，但像小孩子一样简单的快乐，确实离成年人越来越远了。但当我在看到《小屁孩日记》的时候，我却突然间想起了自己童年时那种纯真、简单的生活，这也是我决定买下这本漫画的原因之一。看《小屁孩日记》会让我把自己带回正轨，审核自己，检查一下自己最近的情绪、状况，还是要回到人的根本——开心。

　　我到现在也喜欢随手画一些小屁孩的画像来送给大家，这个也是最近一年来形成的习惯，因为自己大学读的是建筑，平时就喜欢随手画些东西，喜欢上小屁孩之后就开始画里面的人物，别看这个漫画线条简单，但想要用最简单的线条画出漫画里那种可爱的感觉，反而挺花功夫的。除了小屁孩这个主角之外，我最喜欢画的就是他的弟弟。弟弟是个特别爱搞鬼的小孩，而且长着一张让人特别想去捏他的脸。这兄弟俩的故事经常会让我想起我跟我妹妹的关系，我妹妹小时候也总是被我"欺负"，比如捏她的脸啊、整蛊她啊，但如果遇到了外人欺负妹妹，自己绝对是第一个站出来保护她的人。

<u>星期五</u>

学生们通过卷纸事件学到的一点是，无论想要什么，都得自己筹款。

上周学生会就班级筹款一事来了一次"脑力风暴"。副主席希拉里·派因说我们可以组织洗车，书记奥利维娅·戴维斯说我们可以来一次旧货甩卖。

我觉得我们应该卖焦糖爆米花！不过罗利的对讲机开得不够响，大家对我彻底无视。

尤金·埃利斯提议在体育馆搞职业摔跤，贾万·希尔想出摩托特技秀。不过他们互不相让，最后只好折中搞了一个半摩托半摔跤活动。

尤金大概知道得花很大功夫才能把这件事情搞起来，所以他就委托给了副主席希拉里。希拉里组建了筹款委员会，让她的学生会朋友加入。

星期一，希拉里跟学生会汇报，说活动已经安排差不多了，不过筹款委员会对最初想法作了"些许调整"。

不知怎么回事儿，摩托摔跤活动变成了情人节舞会。尤金和其他男生想把活动改回去，但伯奇夫人说大家必须尊重筹款委员会的决定。我确信其实是她自己本来就没兴趣在体育馆搞机动车活动。

情人节舞会的消息自从传出后，就成了大家在学校谈论的唯一话题。女生们好像非常兴奋，她们把这个看成了中学毕业舞会。

学校本来就有个舞蹈委员会，罗利因为是外联部部长所以接到邀请加入。幸好舞蹈委员会上还有几个男生代表，因为女生们要是得逞，克里斯蒂娜①就会成为当晚的主角。

① 译注：在上一册中出现过，一个歌词非常正能量的女歌手，常在各大百货公司演出。

大多数男生对舞会根本不屑一顾。我听到好几个男生说绝对别指望他们会花3美元去学校体育馆跳舞。不过这周刚开始的时候，第一份糖果寄语在年级教室派出来后，情况就陡然一变。

糖果寄语是情人节舞会的邀请函，舞蹈委员不知从哪天在午饭时间开始卖的。只要花25美分，你就可以向任何人发送糖果寄语，布莱斯·安德森立刻就收到了至少五份来自不同女生的糖果寄语。

亲爱的布莱斯：
　　如果你能在情人节与我共舞，这个节日必将无比甜蜜！

杰西卡

第一波糖果寄语送出后，一些没收到寄语的男生开始眼红那些收到的人。突然之间，人人都想去舞会了，因为没人想被落下。昨天午饭时大家开始抢购糖果寄语。

掏裤兜

糖果寄语

我之前就说过，今年我们年级男生比女生多，好些男生担心舞会找不到舞伴，所以女生在旁边的时候，大多数男生开始表现得很不一样。

吃午饭的时候，男生都喜欢用勺子把土豆泥弹到天花板上，看谁的那团能黏住。

你可别问我他们往土豆里加了什么才能让它们这么黏。

黏糊糊

挖一勺　　弹出去

有时候我坐下来之前忘记要先抬头看看。

女生很讨厌土豆泥这个把戏，所以她们都坐在食堂另一边。不过现在男生们都知道如果他们继续混蛋下去就没女生跟他们跳舞了。

可以看得出来，对许多男生来说，在女生面前装成熟是无比难受的。当女生不在旁边的时候，很多男生就开始发泄了。

我们的体育课正上到篮球单元，女生在体育馆的一边，男生在另一边。一天，有个叫安东尼·伦弗鲁的男生贪玩，想着如果在丹尼尔·雷维斯投罚球的时候把他裤子扒掉的话，一定很爆笑。

除了丹尼尔之外，大家都笑了。不过后来安东尼带球上篮的时候，丹尼尔终于以其人之道还治其人之身。之后就彻底失控了，大家开始互相乱扒裤子……从此一切变得惨不忍睹。

现在大家都成了惊弓之鸟，唯恐被扒裤子，结果在篮球练习时大家连站都不敢站起来。

快速平移　快速平移　滚动　快速平移

我甚至还开始在运动裤里面穿两条内裤以求加倍保险。

快速平移

事情一发不可收拾，以至于罗伊副校长今天亲自来到体育馆给男生训话。他说这个绝非玩笑，扒裤者一旦被抓到就作停学处理。

不过罗伊副校长本该先看清他站的位置的，某个男生躲在阶梯看台后面，把他扒了个措手不及。

不知道是谁干的，反正罗伊副校长没抓到他。没人能确定他是谁，江湖上管他叫"扒裤狂人"。

星期二

糖果寄语已经开始快一周了，我一封都还没收到，开始有点慌了。我长这么大还从来没把土豆往天花板上弹过，也从来没有扒过别人的裤子，所以我实在不知道今时今日男生要怎样才能打动女生了。

我们年级教室里好像每个男生都收到糖果寄语了，连特拉维斯·希基都收到了。他这个人，只要你给他一枚25美分硬币，你让他从垃圾箱里捡剩披萨吃他都干。

有一天晚上，盖瑞叔叔在我房里玩电脑游戏，我跟他说了情人节舞会和糖果寄语的事儿。说你也不信，他给的几条建议还真的颇有见地。

盖瑞叔叔说，吸引女生注意的最佳办法就是要显得"高不可攀"。他说我应该去买一堆糖果寄语，然后统统寄给自己，这样女生就会以为我是热门人选。

早该想到跟盖瑞叔叔请教了。他好像都结过四次婚了，绝对是交际老手。

昨天我买了总值两美元的糖果寄语，今天在年级教室里全部收到了。

但愿能成，这两美元可是我的午饭钱啊。

星期五

截至星期三，我已经烧掉五美元了，如果我继续给自己买糖果寄语的话，非得饿死不可。所以我决定，干脆买一个糖果寄语送给女生，看看效果如何。

昨天午饭时，我买了一个糖果寄语送给阿德里安娜·辛普森，她在英语课上座位跟我隔了三排。我不想把25美分全部押在一个人身上，所以我要确定我的钱能值回本。

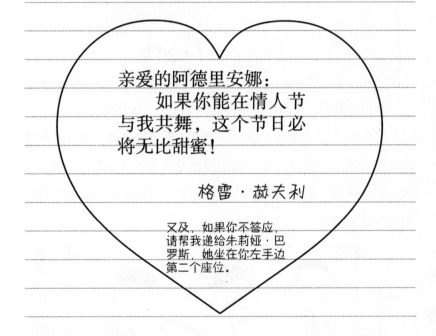

亲爱的阿德里安娜：
　　如果你能在情人节
与我共舞，这个节日必
将无比甜蜜！

格雷·赫夫利

又及，如果你不答应，
请帮我递给朱莉娅·巴
罗斯，她坐在你左手边
第二个座位。

我今天走进课室的时候，阿德里安娜和朱莉娅都瞪了我一眼。所以我猜她们俩都把我给拒绝了。

不过我意识到糖果寄语并非是邀请女生跳舞的唯一方法。有个叫莱安·马洛的女生上历史课时在年级教室里坐在我坐的位置上。所以我就在书桌上给她写了张字条，一分钱也不用花。

可惜我忘记放学留堂同样在历史课教室，所以莱安还没读到我的字条时就有好些白痴抢先答复了。

嗨，莱安——
如果你还在寻觅舞伴的话，回复字条让我知道一下吧。
　　　格雷·赫夫利

嗨，格雷——很抱歉，我无意与你跳舞。
　　　　　莱安

亲爱的格雷：
是的，我愿意跟你去跳舞。还有，你愿意娶我吗？
　　　　哈哈哈

亲亲

我挺紧张的，因为现在好像没剩几个女生可以挑了。

有个女生还没舞伴，她叫埃丽卡·埃尔南德斯。她刚刚和男朋友哈马尔·劳分手，这个男生因为把头卡在椅子里出不来而全校出名。清洁工只好用锯子把椅子锯断才把他救出来。这个都记载到学校年鉴里了。

窘境：哈马尔·劳在莫兰夫人的美术课上把头卡在凳子里，刘易斯先生正在帮忙解围。

埃丽卡长得漂亮，人又好，所以我实在不能理解她是怎么跟哈马尔这种蠢货走到一起的。

她本来会是我的舞伴首选。不过我担心如果我跟她一拍即合，将来我会一直记得她的前男友而无法释怀。

埃丽卡·埃尔南德斯的情况让我不禁考虑其他女生是否也有过一段像埃丽卡与哈马尔·劳那样的交往。很难追踪学校里谁跟谁交往过，不过找舞伴的时候，这个可是重要信息。所以我就画了个图来研究我们年级里的各种关系。

要完全理清不容易，这是目前未完成版本。

我比较担心的是一个叫埃文·怀特黑德的男生。我听他吹嘘过自己亲吻了好些我们年级的不同女生。

不过上周他因为出水痘被送回家了，我都不知道这年头还有人会出水痘啊。所以啊，天晓得有多少女生被传染了。

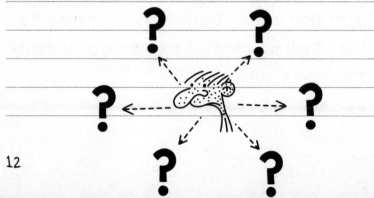

我十分确定有一个女生埃文没有亲过，那就是朱莉·韦伯，因为她从五年级开始就一直在跟埃德·诺韦尔交往。不过我听说他们最近关系摇摇欲坠，所以我打算乘人之危一下。

星期二

盖瑞叔叔跟我说，要是我想找到女生跳舞，我必须当面邀请。虽然我一直都尽量避免跟女生正面交锋，不过我觉得他言之有理。

有个叫佩顿·埃利斯的女生让我一直有点心动，昨天我看她在饮水器喝水，我就站在她旁边耐心等她喝完。不过佩顿肯定是眼角余光看到了我，知道我要邀舞，所以她就一直喝个不停，让我在一旁干等。

最后，上课铃响了，我们俩都得回教室了。

我跟佩顿不太熟，所以邀她跳舞可能比较失策。我还是应该对和我平时有点来往的人下手。我第一个想到的就是贝萨妮·布林，我的自然课实验室搭档。

　　不过我估计我给贝萨妮留下的印象不太好。我们最近在上解剖单元，过去一连几天我们都在解剖青蛙。一看到那些东西我就想吐，所以我就让贝萨妮来解剖，我自己在课室另一边遏制呕吐的冲动。

　　话说回来，今时今日，难道我们还需要把青蛙切开才知道它们肚子里有什么吗？

　　如果有人跟我说青蛙有五脏六腑，我很乐意直接相信。

　　跟贝萨妮成为搭档我还蛮高兴的。我记得上小学的时候，每次有老师让男生和女生搭伴干活儿，班里就会一片哗然。

当老师把我跟贝萨妮凑成一对的时候，我还以为班里会有点动静呢。不过我看大家是长大了，不兴这套了。

虽然我没能以我的解剖技术打动贝萨妮，我觉得我还是有戏的。不是我吹，我可是个很会搞怪的实验室搭档。

昨天放学，贝萨妮从衣物柜里拿大衣的时候，我走到她跟前。

我承认，虽然我们每天在实验室共处45分钟，但跟她说话我还是会有点紧张。我一个字都还没说出来，脑中就开始浮现青蛙。所以估计我跟她是不成了。

　　昨晚我跟盖瑞叔叔讲了学校发生的事儿，他说我败就败在单枪匹马上阵，他说我需要个"托儿"在女生面前给我衬托一下，这样再约女生就容易多了。

　　好吧，我觉得罗利就是个完美的"托儿"，因为他只要本色出演就足以把我衬托出来了。

绊倒

　　今天我叫罗利当我的托儿，但他不太理解"托儿"这个概念。我说这就类似于当我的助选经纪人，不过不是竞选而是找舞伴。

罗利说我们可以互为彼此的托儿，这样大家都能找到舞伴，我说我们得一个一个来。我觉得还是先解决我的问题比较好，因为要帮罗利找到舞伴那可是持久战。

午饭时分，我们小试了一下怎么做托儿，不过我觉得改进空间还很大。

我听说格雷·赫夫利肌肉健美。

星期四

放学回家路上，罗利说舞蹈委员会的一个女生告诉他阿莉莎·格罗夫刚跟男友分手，正在寻觅舞伴。

看吧，这就是为什么我让罗利给我做托儿。阿莉莎是我们学校最红的女生之一，所以我得赶紧行动，以免被班里其他白痴捷足先登。

回家后我就立刻给阿莉莎打了个电话，不过没人接。答录机立刻启用了，我还没反应过来，就进入语音信箱了。

呃……对……我是格……雷·赫夫利……我打电话过来是因为……

我按了"#"字键来删除留言然后重新录音。不过我的第二遍录音还是不怎么样。

嗨，我是格雷·赫夫利，我想找梅利莎，看看她是否有意……

我了个去！

我肯定录了不下20次，因为我想录得恰到好处。不过罗利在房里想保持安静，每次看到他我就忘词儿。

没过多久，我跟罗利开始玩起来，一点正经都没有了。

我知道罗利在我家的时候我是没法正儿八经电话留言的，所以我把最后一条删掉，然后挂了电话。我还是等明天早上跟阿莉莎当面说吧。

不过没想到敲击"#"键在格罗夫家语音信箱系统中并不会删除语音信息，跟我们家的设置不同。晚饭后敲门声大作，原来是阿莉莎的父亲找上门来了。

格罗夫先生跟老爸说我和我的朋友在他们家的答录机上留了20条恶作剧留言，希望我们以后再也不要往他们家打电话。

① 译注：Snarf（怪猫）是上世纪80年代动画片《霹雳猫》（Thundercats），港译《虎威战士》中的角色。

看来只好把阿莉莎从我的舞伴名单上抹掉了。

星期一

　　盖瑞叔叔说如果我想对学校里的女生传递正确的讯息，可以考虑改改我的行头。他说穿新衬衫或新鞋子总能让人倍感自信，他说我不妨试试看。

　　问题是，我就没几件新东西。我敢说我身上穿的90%都是罗德里克的"二手货"。老妈说这言过其实。但只要你看看我内裤后面的标签就知道了。

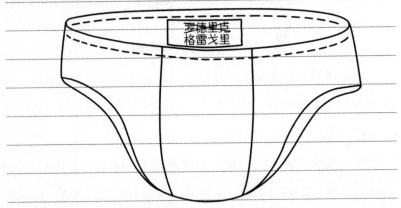

　　我从来不怎么在意穿着，不过既然盖瑞叔叔这么说了，我开始反思是不是衣着拖了我的后腿。

　　周末我问老妈能不能一起去给我买条新牛仔裤和一双新鞋，

这样我可以在学校看起来帅一点。不过话一出口我就后悔了。

老妈给我来了一通长长的训话，说现在的中学生过度重视外表，如果我们能把考虑穿着的时间花一半在学习上，我们的国家就不会在数学世界排名上屈居第25位了。

我就知道老妈不会同意给我买新衣服的。说起来，老妈当年坐镇家长教师联合会的时候，她还发起倡议要推广校服，因为她从某篇文章读到穿校服的孩子学习好。

幸好，她当时没获得足够的签名支持，不过一传十十传百，大家都知道是我妈发起的校服倡议，一连几周我放学都得等上半小时才能安全回家。

因为老妈不肯带我去买衣服，我决定自己解决。我在家里东刨刨西刨刨，看看能不能找到一两件酷一点的东西可以穿。

我先是翻一遍罗德里克的衣橱，不过我觉得我们在衣着品味上完全不搭。

盖瑞叔叔说我可以看看老爸的衣橱，因为有时候大人有些"复古"服装看起来酷酷的。我是从来没见老爸穿过什么跟酷沾边儿的衣服，不过我还是愿意一试。

我还真挺高兴盖瑞叔叔给了我这番提点，因为说来你也不信，我在老爸的衣橱里找到了刚好想找的东西。

一件黑色皮夹克。我从没见过老爸穿过，所以我猜这肯定是老爸在我出生之前买的。

还真没想到老爸会有这么酷的东西，顿时对老爸刮目相看。

我穿上皮夹克走下楼。老爸看到他的旧皮夹克十分惊讶，他说这是他刚开始跟老妈约会时买的。

我问老爸我能不能把夹克借走，他说反正他也不穿了，所以他没意见。

遗憾的是老妈不愿意。她说那件皮夹克对中学生来说太贵了，搞不好我会弄坏或弄丢。

我跟她说这个没道理，因为这夹克放在家里也就是积灰而已，跟坏了、丢了其实没什么区别。老妈说穿皮夹克会传递"错误讯息"，而且大冬天穿不合适。所以她让我把衣服放回楼上衣橱里。

不过我今早洗澡的时候，我满脑子都是把夹克穿去学校后的各种风流倜傥。我知道我可以把衣服从家里"顺"出去，然后再放回衣橱里，这样老妈就什么都不会发现。

老妈给曼尼喂早餐的时候，我就走上楼，拿了夹克然后匆匆从前门出去。

首先我不得不说，老妈说得对，皮夹克的确不能当御寒大衣来穿。

那件夹克一点衬里都没有，上学走到半路我就后悔死了。

我的手套在家里的大衣兜儿里，我手都要冻僵了。所以我就把手揣进皮夹克兜儿里，不过两个兜儿里都有东西。

一边口袋摸到一副超酷的飞行员墨镜，又添一员。另一个兜里摸到一组照相间里拍出的照片。

一开始我还没认出照片里的人，后来才意识到这就是老爸和老妈。

刚吃完早饭就看到这种照片……

等我到学校的时候，我在走廊里回头率为百分之百。

得到如此多的关注，我决定一整天都不脱夹克了。在年级教室里我简直成了全新的一个人。

就在上课铃响前几分钟，有人大力地敲门上的小·窗格。

看到是谁敲门后我简直要发心脏病了。

老师打开了门，老妈径直朝我走来，让我当着大家的面交出老爸的皮夹克。

我跟老妈说外面太冷，没有皮夹克没法回家，老妈就把自己的大衣给了我。

情况并不如意，不过我好歹回家路上不冷了。

星期三

现在学校里人人都知道有人被迫穿老妈的大衣。这样一来，我要找舞伴又难上加难了。

所以我认为我还是找个外校的女生来跳舞比较有机会。而且我已经知道从哪儿找最合适了——教会。

我听说上教会学校的孩子觉得上公立学校的孩子都很强。所以每次在教会遇到我的朋友，我都在教会学校的孩子面前尽可能耍酷。

最近，老妈跟教会的斯特林格太太熟络起来，因为她们都在秋交会委员会干过。

斯特林格一家有两个孩子都在读教会学校，男孩叫韦斯利，女孩叫劳蕾尔。我从未见过韦斯利，所以他一定是在礼拜的时候跟其他小孩一起呆在地下室。

斯特林格先生　　劳蕾尔·斯特林格　　斯特林格太太

几天前，老妈邀请了斯特林格全家这周五来我们家共进晚餐。我看老妈是希望曼尼和韦斯利可以来电，这样曼尼可以第一次跟活人交朋友。

不过我发现我有一个绝佳的机会。劳蕾尔跟我同年级，而且比我们班的大多数女生都好看。所以这顿晚饭可能会让我时来运转。

星期五

老妈在斯特林格一家来之前，花了好长时间才把房子收拾好。我四处看了看，觉得还是插手一下比较好。

到处都是让人尴尬的东西。首先，我们的圣诞树还立在客厅里。要把它拆卸开来实在太费事儿，我跟老爸就干脆把它塞到车库去了。

啪嗒

娱乐室里，每件家具的四个角上都还残留着纸尿裤。这些是当年曼尼开始爬的时候，老妈为了避免曼尼碰头而贴到家具上的。

老妈用的是封箱透明胶，那玩意儿还真不好弄下来。

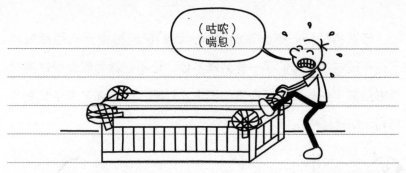

（咕哝）
（喘息）

　　盖瑞叔叔正在娱乐室的沙发上打盹，所以我们就用被单把他盖起来，希望不要有人坐上去。

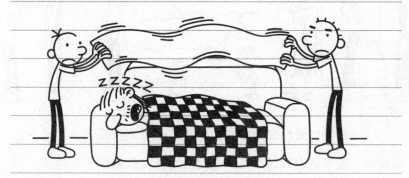

ZZZZZ

　　下一步就是厨房。墙上有个公告板贴了还有各种证书和彩带，都是这些年来老妈给我们颁发的。

　　凡是写着我名字的东西都很窘，所以我就把公告板从墙上拿下来藏到食物间去了。

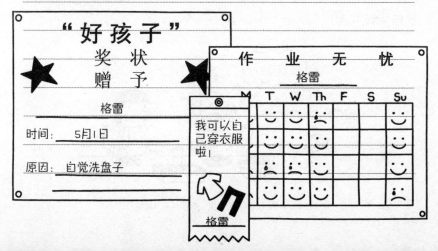

"好孩子"
奖　状
赠　予

格雷

时间：　5月1日

原因：　自觉洗盘子

作　业　无　忧
格雷

M	T	W	Th	F	S	Su
⌣	⌣	⌣	⌢			⌣
⌣	⌣	⌣	⌣			
⌣	⌣	⌣	⌣			⌣
	⌣	⌣	⌣			⌢

我可以自己穿衣服啦！

格雷

等斯特林格一家出现的时候，我们已经把重大问题都解决了。不过这次会客似乎一开头就不妙。记不记得我跟你说过曼尼很害怕某个在教会扮吸血鬼的男生？好吧，原来那个男生就是韦斯利·斯特林格。

所以老妈对曼尼交新朋友的寄望算是付诸东流了。曼尼不肯吃晚饭，整个晚上躲在卧室，要是我也能借故躲起来就好了，因为老妈做了一顿丰盛的饭菜来招待我们的客人。

奶油香菇鸡块配芦笋。我也知道芦笋对身体有益，可是芦笋偏偏是我的氪石①。

我不想在劳蕾尔面前失礼，所以我决定闭上眼睛捏住鼻子，然后生吞下去。

① 译注：kryptonite，氪石，超人的克星，能使其失去超能力。

大人们都在聊政治和其他无趣的东西，我跟劳蕾尔只好在一边坐着听。

老妈跟斯特林格太太讲她跟老爸"约会之夜"去的高级餐厅，斯特林格太太说她和她丈夫周末从来不出去吃饭，因为劳蕾尔老是跟朋友们出去，而他们一直无法为韦斯利找到可靠的保姆。

我自告奋勇跟斯特林格太太说，如果他们需要保姆，只管找我就好。

我觉得这是跟斯特林格一家熟络起来的办法，而且还有钱拿，何乐不为。老妈也很赞成，因为她觉得带小孩的经验对我来说很有意义。斯特林格太太似乎被说动了，她问我明天是否有空，我说有空。

我也不想把话说太满，不过我确定迟早有一天我会在感恩节坐在斯特林格一家人旁边，一起笑着细数我中学时怎样照顾我小舅子。

星期六

晚上6：30老妈把我送到了斯特林格家。

斯特林格太太说劳蕾尔已经去了朋友家，这太没劲了，我还想跟她聊几分钟，说说舞会的事儿呢。

斯特林格太太让我8：00哄韦斯利上床睡觉，他们大概9：00到家，还说我在他们回来之前可以随意看电视，冰箱里的东西随意取用。

斯特林格夫妇走后，就只剩下我和韦斯利了。我问韦斯利要不要玩棋盘游戏之类的，他说他想去车库拿他的自行车。

我跟他说外面太冷了，不宜骑自行车，但他说他想在室内骑。斯特林格一家的房子还真不错，我确信他们不想让韦斯利把硬木地板刮花，所以我跟他说我们得找点儿别的事儿干。

韦斯利大发雷霆。等他冷静下来后，他说他想填色。我问他填色工具在哪儿，他说在洗衣间里。不过等我进了洗衣间去拿，我听到门闩从门后插上了。

然后我听到车库门打开，紧接着韦斯利就在厨房骑上了自行车。
我大力拍门让他放我出来，但他就是无视我。

然后我听到地下室的门开了，一连串隆隆声，紧接是一次猛烈碰撞。我可以听到韦斯利在楼梯下面哭，我开始慌了，因为听上去他好像真的很疼。

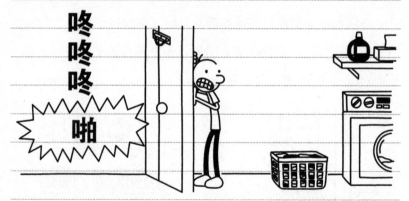

不过等韦斯利平静下来，我听到他拖着自行车回到楼上。然后他沿着楼梯往下骑，又一路滚到楼下，然后哭得死去活来。

就这么反反复复有一个半小时，我真的没有夸张。我以为韦斯利总会有疲惫的时候，但他完全没有。我记得斯特林格夫妇说他们没法给韦斯利找到保姆，我现在总算明白了。

我一离开洗衣房就一定要好好治一下韦斯利。他绝对该打屁股，不过斯特林格夫妇肯定不同意。

我决定罚韦斯利闭门思过，因为我小时候不乖的时候我爸妈也这么对我。其实，我小时候还被罗德里克罚过面壁。

当时我不知道罗德里克根本无权让我面壁思过。罗德里克带我的时候，我都不知道在思过椅上度过了多少时光。

有一次我跟罗德里克单独在家，我在屋子里扔球，不小心砸碎了老爸跟老妈的结婚照。罗德里克因为这个罚我面壁半小时。

老爸老妈回家后，他们看到照片摔坏了，问是我们俩谁干的。我说是我干的，不过他们不用罚我了，因为罗德里克已经罚过我面壁了。

不过老妈说唯一有权处罚的就只有她和老爸。结果因为打碎了那幅照片，我被罚面壁两次。

扫扫

韦斯利把我锁在洗衣房里，就为这个罚他面壁三次都不为过。不过已经不早了，如果斯特林格夫妇回到家时我还被锁在里面，那就面子上挂不住了。

所以我开始另外想办法出去。有一台闲置的冰箱堵住了通往房子后面的门。我费了九牛二虎之力，推出一个足够大的空隙让我刚好可以钻出去开门。

外面冷死了，我只穿了件T恤衫和一条裤子。我试图打开前门，但发现被锁住了。

我决定出新招让他猝不及防。我绕房子走，试遍了所有窗子终于找到一个没锁的。然后我把窗子推开，爬了进去。

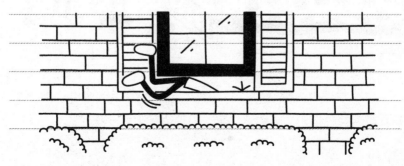

我头先着地，掉进了某人的卧室，我四处看了看，发现这一定是劳蕾尔的卧室。

刚才说过，外面天寒地冻，所以我需要先暖和一下再去治韦斯利。不过我相当后悔我当时花了几分钟时间来取暖，因为正当我在劳蕾尔房里的时候，斯特林格夫妇回到家了。

但愿将来某个感恩节，我们可以一起笑对这段往事。不过我猜要等斯特林格先生笑对这件事，恐怕得等上好一阵了。

星期三

　　跟劳蕾尔·斯特林格的希望化成泡影后，我基本上放弃了找舞伴的想法。还剩三天了，现在大家基本上都已经成双成对了。我还是周六晚上一个人在家落寞地打电动游戏好了。

　　不过昨天罗利参加完舞蹈委员会会议后跟我说了一则消息，彻底改变了一切。

　　他说阿比吉尔·布朗在会上情绪低落，因为她的舞伴迈克尔·桑普森家里有事儿所以临时取消了。现在阿比吉尔徒有舞裙没有舞伴。

　　看来我英雄救美的时刻到了。我告诉罗利，这就是他给我做托儿，撮合我和阿比吉尔的大好机会。

　　问题是阿比吉尔并不认识我，我有点怀疑她是否愿意跟一个素不相识的人去跳舞。所以我跟罗利说他不妨先跟阿比吉尔说我们三人组成"好友团"一起去跳舞。

罗利觉得这主意不错，因为他一直忙于舞蹈委员会的工作，也没找到舞伴。

我盘算着要是我们三人能共进晚餐，阿比吉尔就能在餐厅里发现我有多好。等走进舞场的时候，我们就已然成双对了。

碰杯

唯一的问题是我们需要搭便车。我没打算让老妈帮忙，因为我们家的小货车座位上全是麦片碎渣，还有些天晓得是什么东西。另外我的约会如果有老妈在场，必定完蛋。

时间过得真快啊，感觉昨天格雷还穿着纸尿裤呢！

我知道如果我真想打动阿比吉尔的话，我可以租一辆豪华加长礼宾车，不过那玩意儿太烧钱了。我忽然灵光一闪。

罗利他爹的车不错，我们可以让他搭我们去。阿比吉尔甚至不需要知道杰弗逊先生就是罗利他爹。如果我们什么都不说，她就会以为他是个专业司机。或许我可以给他弄一顶司机礼帽，来强化这一印象。

当然，我们同样什么都不能跟杰弗逊先生说。我跟他以前有点过节，我确定他不会乐意为我额外帮忙的。

事情开始就绪了。罗利跟阿比吉尔说了，阿比吉尔支持"好友团"这个点子。另外，杰弗逊先生也答应开车送我们去舞会了。

我现在就只求从现在到周六晚不要出什么事儿把事情搅黄。

星期五

我跟盖瑞叔叔说了舞会的事儿，他看起来好像比我还兴奋。他想知道所有细节，比如有多少人参加，有没有请唱片骑师。不过我不知道怎么回答，因为罗利才是舞蹈委员会的人，这些事儿归他的部门管。

我更关心穿什么。盖瑞叔叔说我要是想打动舞伴就得穿西装。我去罗德里克的柜子里翻出了一套他出席盖瑞叔叔某次婚礼时穿过的西装。

我在罗德里克的杂物抽屉里没找到古龙水，不过却找到了一瓶电视广告上常见的身体喷雾。我不大敢用，因为如果真的像广告那么灵的话，明晚就会成为我的噩梦。

尖叫！

我的舅公布鲁斯几年前去世了，我知道车库里还有一箱他的遗物。我找到了一瓶他用过的古龙水，在手腕上喷了一些。

用完之后，我闻起来跟舅公布鲁斯一模一样，不过我觉得还是比用那瓶身体喷雾来得安全。

我还让老爸带我去杂货店给阿比吉尔买了一盒情人节巧克

力。我实在不应该把盒子上的塑封撕掉的，因为我已经把牛油忌廉、花生蘸和焦糖味儿的吃掉了。

但愿阿比吉尔喜欢椰子味儿的和另一种牙膏味儿的，因为只剩这几种了。

星期六

今晚就是盛大的情人节舞会之夜，开头就不顺。

我去罗利家做准备的时候，我发现他脸上有红点点就像蚊子咬过留下的包。然后我猛然意识到，这些点点是：水痘。

自从埃文·怀特黑德几周前出了水痘，水痘就像野火一样在班里蔓延。

上周有四个男生被校医送回家了。我确定他们四个里面肯定有一个就是"扒裤狂人"，因为自从周二之后就再没发生过扒裤事件。

我听说水痘超级容易传染，一旦有人得了水痘就一周不准上学。不过我可容不得罗利缺席。他是我的舞会车票，而且我知道如果他爸妈不让他去，那我也去不成了。

我告诉罗利他得了水痘，不过我不该这么简单粗暴，本该采用更温婉的方式的。

罗利本来要径直下楼去告诉他爸妈，不过我让他先冷静，说我们一起想办法。

我说如果他能坚持完今晚，不告诉任何人，我这辈子都欠他的。他只需要掩盖一下他的水痘，不要跟爸妈大嘴巴就行了。我们一起去舞会，好好享受，不许要任何人知道。

不过罗利太慌了，已经无法思考了，所以我只好给他两块椰子味儿巧克力来让他冷静下来。

罗利知道自己得了水痘之后，就开始痒个不停了。所以我从他的梳妆台拿出袜子套在他手上。

我猜罗利的爸妈大概知道水痘长什么样，我们得找个办法掩盖一下。我们去了他父母的洗手间，翻了他母亲的化妆盒，看有没有什么可以能用的。我找到一种叫"遮瑕膏"的东西，听起来似乎合用。

我用抽屉里找到的一把小刷子来涂抹罗利脸上的问题区域。

不过一眼就能看出罗利化了妆。所以我从杰弗逊太太的梳妆台上拿了一条丝巾，让罗利围上丝巾，罩住嘴的周围。然后我发现他额头也有几粒，所以我又从他母亲的柜子里找到一顶沙滩帽，让他把帽子也戴上。

　　不敢说罗利看上去与常人无异，不过好歹看不出他有水痘。

　　当我们上车的时候，我都快要摒住呼吸了，不过我猜杰弗逊先生以为罗利的打扮是某种中学时尚，所以他什么都没说。

　　当我打开后门上车的时候，看到罗利的儿童座占了一个位置我还有点吃惊。

我问罗利为何他还用儿童座，他说他们就是一直没拿下来，虽然他已经不需要用儿童座了。怪不得每次罗利坐他们家车经过时，我都觉得他好像太高了点儿。

我知道我们去接阿比吉尔之前必须把那玩意儿拿掉，因为豪华加长礼宾车公司是绝对不会在车上安儿童座的。

不过那座子扣得很死，非得工程师出马才能知道怎么把它卸下来。那会儿我们已经晚了，所以只好随它去了。

我们在阿比吉尔家的车道上停下之后，我让杰弗逊先生鸣笛示意我们已经到了。

不过杰弗逊先生不肯鸣笛，他说这样对待一位"淑女"有违绅士之道。他说必须由我们两人之一去前门"护送"她。

罗利正要出去，不过我意识到这是我的一大良机，可以借此给阿比吉尔一个良好的第一印象。所以我就走到房前敲门去了。

不过阿比吉尔没有来前门开门——她爹出来了。显然，布朗先生是个州骑警，除非他本人喜好化妆成骑警。

布朗先生说阿比吉尔还在楼上准备，随时下来。

他让我进来坐着等。我感觉我们俩坐着等阿比吉尔下楼等了一个小时，布朗先生皮带上的手铐让我浑身不自在。

我终于决定，为了这个情人节舞会，真没必要受这么大罪，就准备撤了。我正准备离开，阿比吉尔就下楼了。

我首先注意到的是阿比吉尔穿了条很蓬松的裙子，我知道我们是不可能三个人一起挤在后座了。不过我绝对不肯坐罗利的儿童座，所以我自告奋勇要坐副驾位置。我还知道杰弗逊先生的前座有自动加热，所以我也不妨一并享用。

　　杰弗逊先生的副驾座位上放了一堆文件，我猜他是准备等我们跳舞的时候在车里报税什么的。

　　要把东西全部搬开太费事儿了，所以我决定在车后面将就一下算了，这样活动才能继续。

　　阿比吉尔好像不太介意罗利坐儿童座，我确信她以为罗利这么做是在开玩笑。

　　不过幽默是我的看家本领，我可不能让罗利抢了我的风头。

车里太安静了，所以我问杰弗逊先生能不能把广播打开。不过他没放音乐，却调到了无聊的访谈广播节目，我们就只好一路听这个。

我确信他故意这么干为了报复我，因为我管他叫"司机"。

罗利和阿比吉尔聊了起来，不过因为我就坐在音箱旁边，听不清他们在说什么。

杰弗逊把车停下来的时候，我还以为我们到了餐厅。结果是

停在一家维修铺门前，为了取回杰弗逊先生的吸尘器。

到了这会儿我就后悔没狠狠心花钱租加长礼宾车了，因为一个专业司机是不会在前往餐厅的路上顺道做其他事情的。

我已经在斯佩里各餐厅订好位置了。这就是老爸老妈常提起的那家高档餐厅。我知道这里价格略高，不过我因为平时做家务已经有了一定积蓄，而且我很想在阿比吉尔面前充充大款。

我们在停车场停下来后，杰弗逊先生为我打开后背箱。我出来时才发现我的西装上沾满了吸尘器上的油污。

我不想被当作是流浪汉，所以我就把西装上衣搁车里，然后一起去了餐厅。我还指望罗利能识趣跟他爸呆一块儿，可是他跟了过来。

斯佩里各餐厅比我想象中高档得多。我们走进去的时候，侍应跟我们说这里是高档餐厅，男士必须穿着外套。

不过我打死也不要穿那脏兮兮的西装外衣，所以我就问侍应能否破例一次。他说不能破例，不过餐厅有一件外套可以借给我。他给我的那件稍大，不过我还是穿上了。

坐下之后我闻到一大股怪味儿，接着一直想搞清楚怪味儿从哪儿来。后来我才意识到这是从我身上传来的。我肯定有不下百人穿过这件公共外套，而且一次都没洗过。

在席间我不想自己身体闻上去有别人的体味，所以我借故去了洗手间，用肥皂和水刷了一下这件外套的腋下部位，然后用干手机来烘干。

结果情况更糟，热气活化了臭味，气味四散开去。

我忍无可忍了。我跟阿比吉尔和罗利说这地方是骗钱的，我们还是撤吧。

我把外套还给了侍应，然后我们三个从大门走出去。我说不如晚餐免了直接去舞会吧，但阿比吉尔说她饿坏了，罗利说他也饿得不行。

斯佩里各

附近就只剩老麦家常菜了，我跟他们说，要我去那儿门都没有。不过罗利说他喜欢老卖家的甜食部，阿比吉尔也说听上去不错。

我开始极度后悔这次约会把罗利带上了，因为他就知道站在阿比吉尔一边。每次投票我都是一比二落败。不过我不想在约会中小题大做，所以就忍忍算了，我们走了三条街来到老麦家。

幸好我还记得前门进去要剪领带的事儿，所以我在最后一秒把我的领带塞进了我的后兜儿。

不过我没来得及警告罗利，现在他的领带成了耻辱之墙的永恒一部分。

老麦家简直就是个动物园。我们家通常是在工作日晚上来，不过到了星期六，这里完全变了样。

好消息是，因为我们没带小孩子来，他们没把我们领到儿童区。不过老麦家的成人区也没好多少。只有几块玻璃把儿童区和成人区分开，我们旁边那家有一堆特别野的小孩儿。

我问服务员能不能换一桌，她摆了一副臭脸，然后把我们的东西挪到了另一桌。不过我真后悔没呆在刚才那桌，因为新的情况根本算不上是改善。

我不敢再让服务员给我们换桌子了，因为最怕的就是把给你端饭的人惹毛了，后果不堪设想。我就找了几份菜单挡住窗户来阻挡视线。

服务员给我们端来了玉米脆片，罗利把手套脱下来以便吃东西。因为罗利得了水痘，跟他从同一个盘子里拿食物恐怕不太好，所以我就把盘子放到我这边。

每次罗利看起来想吃脆片的样子，我就用吸管推一片过去。

滑动

我记不清水痘是不是空气传播的了，所以每次罗利说话我都屏住呼吸。

嗯呃哼呼

有一次他讲了一件去年夏天发生的事情，故事太长，到最后我几乎要窒息了。

这就是为什么我们家再也不会租那间沙滩小屋了！

喘气！

我告诉阿比吉尔和罗利，说今晚我做东，他们想吃什么就点什么。我想四处挥霍一下，在阿比吉尔面前稍微摆摆阔。

　　不过等服务员回来的时候，阿比吉尔点了两份小菜，罗利也一样。

　　服务员不知道罗利在说什么，因为他隔着围巾讲话。于是罗利把围巾拉下来。就在他扯下围巾的那一刻，一点唾沫星子飞溅过来，正好落在我的下唇上。

　　我把下巴完全放松，以防那点唾沫星子滑进我嘴里。我尽量外表装得淡定，但其实我内里已经完全惊慌失措了。

　　我想拿餐巾纸来擦，不过我之前把餐巾纸掉地上了，够不着。所以我就趁阿比吉尔不注意时在她袖子上蹭了一下。

我们点了菜，我要了一份原味汉堡来省钱。阿比吉尔要了一份T骨牛排，这是菜单上最贵的菜，而且尽管我示意罗利找便宜的来点，他还是点了跟阿比吉尔一样的。

菜端上来的时候，我的汉堡里头有生菜和西红柿，老麦家经常搞错顾客点的菜。我把生菜和西红柿拿掉，但上面还有蛋黄酱。

服务员走过来的时候，我跟她说我点的是原味汉堡什么都不加的。她就拿了一块餐巾纸，当着我们的面把蛋黄酱抹掉。

我看了之后就完全没胃口了。不过就算我真的很饿，我也不会把东西全部吃掉。因为如果你把东西吃干净，你就会看到老麦家的盘子有个图，我真心看不下去。

　　我就坐在那儿等阿比吉尔和罗利把牛扒吃完，等他们吃完后，我示意服务员过来结帐。

　　不过罗利和阿比吉尔说他们还想吃甜品。我们之所以来老麦家就是冲着它的甜食部——餐后甜点是免费的。不过罗利和阿比吉尔都想点菜单上的专供甜点，这些需要额外付费。

我起身跟服务员说今天是罗利的生日，因为我知道这样罗利就可以得到免费甜点。几分钟后，服务员齐齐出动端着免费蛋糕过来给罗利唱"生日快乐"。

阿比吉尔还是点了一个三层巧克力芝士蛋糕，不过她只吃了两口。

账单送到的时候，我简直难以置信。我把我钱包里的钱全花光了，连我藏在袜子里的最后5块钱救命钱都拿出来了。

服务员不肯收我从袜子里掏出来的钱，因为有点湿。所以我只好走到杰弗逊先生停车的地方问他有没有5块钱可以跟我换。

等我回来的时候，罗利和阿比吉尔聊得正欢，看上去他们好像比我出去的时候坐得更近了。

我本想给阿比吉尔提个醒，让她对罗利保持距离。不过我担心她听到水痘之后就立刻落跑。

我们三个回到车上，杰弗逊先生把我们送到学校，在大门口把我们放下来。他给了罗利一个深情拥抱，如果阿比吉尔真的以为他是专业司机的话，肯定迷惑死了。

舞会的主题是"午夜巴黎"，不得不承认舞蹈委员会干得不错。

体育馆经过一番布置，看上去就像一条巴黎的街道。有一条长长的桌子，上面有潘趣酒和零食，还有一个用草莓来蘸的巧克力喷泉。

我们交出门票，然后就排队拍照了。每对舞伴都可以在巴黎布景前拍照。

轮到我们的时候，我跟阿比吉尔站在一起，摄影师给我们拍了照片。不过我要是早知道罗利要来掺和，那就干脆不拍为好。

午夜巴黎
情人节舞会

唱片骑师看上去有点眼熟，等我走近再看，发现竟是盖瑞叔叔。你可别问我他是怎么搞到这份工作的。

盖瑞叔叔肯定是看准了这个机会来卖他的T恤衫。体育馆里黑灯瞎火的，孩子们不知道自己被坑了。

前一分钟阿比吉尔还站在我身边，后一分钟就不见人了。我终于在体育馆另一边看到了她，她正在和朋友们聊天。

我朝她们走过去，但我还没走到，她们就一块儿进了女洗手间。

我实在搞不懂女生为什么要成群结队去上洗手间，不过她们这会儿上洗手间倒让我莫名紧张。

我还不知道阿比吉尔对我印象如何，不过我猜她肯定会立刻跟她的朋友们说。男洗手间就在女洗手间隔壁，所以我进了男洗手间，把耳朵紧贴墙壁。

我可以听到她们的阵阵笑声，但听不清说话内容，因为男洗手间里不停传来喧响。

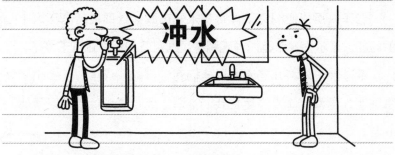

　　我想让大家别发出噪音，但效果不大。

　　墙的另一面安静了下来，所以我赶紧回到体育馆，阿比吉尔和她的朋友们正在潘趣酒旁边。

　　7：50分，盖瑞叔叔把音量调大，看来舞会即将正式开始。不过就在这会儿，一群爷爷奶奶级的人开始陆续进场。

到了9：00入口处就有上百号人了。老师们和几个老年人起了争执，我走近围观。

老年人声称他们订了体育馆来开市政会议商量新老年人中心的问题。希尔夫人跟她们说她两个星期前就把体育馆订下来了。

不过那帮老头儿老太太说他们两个月前就订了，还拿出了文书证明。这群老年人说要把我们这群小屁孩清出体育馆以便他们开会。

然后几个舞蹈委员会的女生开始插嘴，看来事态要开始演变得不堪入目了。

就在大战即将爆发之际，希尔夫人提出折中方案。她说我们可以把体育馆对半分开，老年人可以在一边开会，孩子们在另一边跳舞。

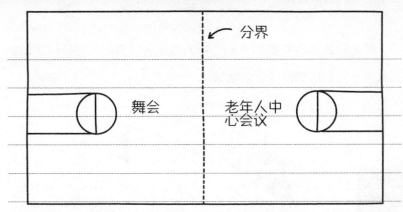

大家都觉得这个方法可以接受，清洁工就把中间的铁栅栏拉了起来。

失掉半壁舞场挺没劲的。不过最扫兴的还是灯光。顶灯只有一个开关，要么全开要么全关。老年人要开灯来开会，这就表示我们这半边"午夜巴黎"的脉动要结束了。

亮光对盖瑞叔叔也很不利，因为所有买了T恤衫的孩子知道自己上当了，会纷纷过来要求退款。

盖瑞叔叔把音量调大，试图分散大家注意力，好些人开始起舞了。

一大群女生们在体育馆中央一起跳舞。偶尔有男生想加入进去，不过都被女生们围起的一堵墙挡在外面了。我之前不理解，直到我试图闯进圈子才发现被彻底阻拦在外。

有一个老年人跑到我们这边来抱怨音乐太响，要求我们调低音量。

盖瑞叔叔把音量调低了近80%，然后我们就连老年人中心会议发言的每一个字都听得清清楚楚的了。

不过这倒没怎么影响女生。她们好些人拿出自己的音乐播放器然后继续跳舞。

不过到那会儿，大多数男生的忍耐都已经到达极限了。一直在女生面前保持规规矩矩可是有代价的，这会儿好些人已经彻底疯狂了。

希尔夫人和其他辅导老师试图安抚男生，但是完全无望。场面极度混乱，而且有点危险。

我还想到阶梯看台那儿去，免得挡别人的路，不过就在那一刻，扒裤狂人再次出手，我决定还是站在原地好些。

每隔一会儿就会有些迟到的人进场，然后看到体育馆内状况后就转身离去。不过就在7：00左右，迈克尔·桑普森和谢丽·贝朗格手牵手走了进来。

迈克尔原本是阿比吉尔的舞伴，看来"家里有事儿"纯属谎言。

从他脸上的表情看来，我猜他也没料到阿比吉尔会出现。

之后就是各种狗血。迈克尔转身离去，把舞伴丢在一边，阿比吉尔在体育馆一角以泪洗面，足足有半个小时。

我尽所能来安慰阿比吉尔，不过她身边有一大群人，我不确定她有没有注意到我。

就在那会儿，老年人中心会议结束，几个老年人开始往我们这边来，自顾自地吃起点心来。

他们很快就把草莓解决掉了，之后巧克力喷泉就没东西可以蘸了。

孩子们开始直接把手伸进巧克力喷泉，老麦家一幕再度上演。

有个男生把隐形眼镜掉到巧克力喷泉里了，希尔夫人让大家站到一边，这样她好等巧克力喷泉循环一圈后再浮出来。

因为会议结束了，盖瑞叔叔就把音量重新调大了。

然后老年人就开始点歌了，不知不觉间，我们的情人节舞会被老年人占领了。

我就靠着墙，看着这一切演变，思索我当初为什么会想来。我也开始后悔没喷罗德里克杂物抽屉里的香喷雾，因为舅公布鲁斯的古龙水吸引来的女生都不是我这个年龄段的。

临近10:00，盖瑞叔叔宣布下一首曲子将是今晚最后一首。音乐响起，孩子们配成对儿双双走向舞池，这还是整晚的第一次。

　　我迫不及待要等这首曲子结束，因为这次舞会就是场灾难，我只想回家打打电动游戏，把这次经历从我脑中抹去。

　　正当我觉得事情已经糟得不能更糟的时候，我看到露比·伯德正朝我走来。

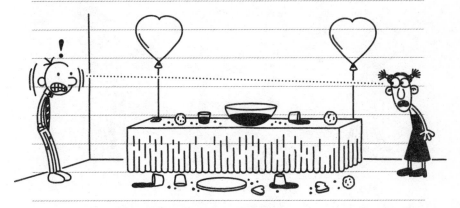

　　我不知道她是要找我跳舞，还是我做了什么把她惹毛了，但我可不想在中学的舞会上以被咬收场。

　　我想方设法要逃脱，但被困住了。所幸的是阿比吉尔就在那一刻从洗手间出来，我在露比抓住我之前，一把拉住阿比吉尔的手。

阿比吉尔的妆已经哭花了，不过我并不在乎。我暗自庆幸有借口让我可以逃脱露比。老实说，我觉得阿比吉尔见到我也挺高兴的，所以我就把她带到舞池的一处空位。

我还从来没跟女生慢舞过，所以我不知道手该往哪儿放。她把手搭在我肩膀，我把手插在裤兜里，不过感觉有点傻。最后我们折中了一下，感觉差不多了。

然后我注意到了阿比吉尔的下巴上有东西。一个小红点点，跟罗利的水痘一模一样。

现在，在我继续讲下去之前，请容我自我辩解一下，我本来就因为水痘的事情快精神崩溃了。

不过我承认，我或许有点反应过头。

原来不是水痘，只是青春痘而已。肯定是阿比吉尔哭的时候，脸上的妆流到下巴上了。

反正现在是知道了，不过在那时的情景下，任何人都会跟我有同样反应的。

不过阿比吉尔估计不这么想，因为回家路上她不怎么搭理我。

我们在阿比吉尔家停下，罗利把她送到家门口。我完全无所谓，刚好可以把剩下的巧克力吃完。经历了这么一番夜晚，我简直要饿死了。

星期三

　　情人节舞会之后发生了很多事。

　　几天前盖瑞叔叔用卖T恤衫的钱买了一堆刮彩彩票，其中一张中了4万美元。他把欠老爸的钱还清，祝我"情场"走运，然后搬出了我们家。

　　另一个消息是我全面爆发水痘。

我没法确定水痘是怎么得来的，不过我真心希望不是从罗利那儿传染来的，因为我一想到如果是罗利的病毒细胞来攻击我的免疫系统，心里就腻歪。

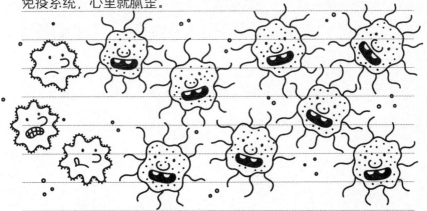

我十分确定不是从罗利那儿得的水痘。前几天我看到他走路上学，他还在下巴上涂他母亲的化妆品。所以我觉得那些红点点肯定是青春痘，就跟阿比吉尔的一样。

说起罗利和阿比吉尔，听说他们两个现在成了一对儿。我只能说，如果这是真的，那罗利就是史上最糟糕的托儿。

我看我可以至少一周不用上学了。好消息是大家都不在家，我可以安心泡澡没人打扰了。

不过我得承认在水里泡着并没我印象中那么舒服，泡了一个小·时就浑身起褶子了。所以我真不知道那9个月是怎么过来的。

而且一整天就我一个人还真有点寂寞（至少我以为屋子里只有我一个人）。今天我在浴缸边上放了条新毛巾，等我睁开眼睛的时候，毛巾不见了。

要么就是有人跟我捣乱，要么就是约翰尼·切达①作祟了。

---

① 译注：约翰尼·切达是上一册中的人物——曼尼有社交障碍，却有一堆"隐形"朋友，约翰尼·切达是其中最爱捣乱的一个。

致　谢

感谢我的妻子茱莉，没有她的爱护与支持，这些书就不可能出版。感谢我的家人：我的妈妈、爸爸、雷、史考特，还有帕特；另外我还想感谢我的大家庭：金尼一家、库里安一家、约翰逊一家、菲奇一家、肯尼迪一家以及伯德特一家。谢谢你们一路支持我，能与你们分享这段创作小说的经历十分有趣。

还要一如既往地感谢我的编辑查理·科赫曼，他让这本小说有机会出版；感谢詹森·威尔斯，他是业内最棒的宣传总监；同时也感谢Abrams出版社的一众同仁。

谢谢我的老板杰斯·贝利尔，以及我在家庭教育网站的同事们。

感谢来自好莱坞的莱利、希维尔、卡拉、尼娜、布拉德、伊丽莎白和基斯。

感谢梅尔·奥顿为前两本书写的书评，实在是精彩得让我受宠若惊了。

谢谢亚伦·尼科迪默斯对我的鼓励，是他让我在已经放弃漫画创作的情况下，重新拾起了画笔。

作者简介

杰夫·金尼是网站Poptropica.com的创始人，凭《小·屁孩日记》、《小·屁孩日记：罗德里克的法则》、《小·屁孩日记：自己动手写日记》登上《纽约时报》畅销作家榜首位。他在华盛顿度过自己的童年，在1995年搬到了新英格兰。杰夫现在住在马萨诸塞州南部，与他的妻子茱莉和两个儿子威尔、格兰特一同生活。

DIARY
of a
Wimpy Kid

by Jeff Kinney

TO GRAM

<u>Friday</u>

I think what the students learned from the toilet paper experience is that if we want something, we're gonna have to raise the money on our own.

So last week the student council brainstormed ideas for a class fundraiser. The Vice President, Hillary Pine, said we should have a car wash, and the Secretary, Olivia Davis, said we should do a giant yard sale.

I thought we should sell caramel popcorn, but either Rowley didn't have his walkie-talkie up loud enough or everybody was just ignoring me.

CARAMEL POPCORN! CARAMEL POPCORN! IS THIS THING ON?

Eugene Ellis suggested a pro wrestling match in the gym, and Javan Hill came up with the idea of a motocross stunt show. But they couldn't decide which idea they liked better, so they settled on a mixed motocross/wrestling event.

I think Eugene realized it was gonna take a lot of work to pull something like that off, so he assigned it to his Vice President. Hillary formed a Fundraising Committee and got her friends on the student council to join it.

On Monday, Hillary reported back to the student council and said that everything for

the event was planned but that the Fundraising
Committee had made a few "small changes" to the
original idea.

Somehow the motocross/wrestling event morphed
into a VALENTINE'S DAY dance. Eugene
and the other guys wanted to change it back,
but Mrs. Birch said they had to respect the
decision of the Fundraising Committee. I'm sure
the truth is that she wasn't really crazy about
the idea of motorized vehicles in the gym to
begin with.

Ever since word got out about the Valentine's Day
dance, it's all anyone can talk about at school.
The girls seem really excited, and they're treating
it like some sort of middle school prom.

There's already a Dance Committee, which
Rowley got invited to be on since he's the Social
Chairperson. I'm just glad there's some male
representation on that committee, because if
the girls have their way, Krisstina will be the
entertainment for the night.

Most of the boys couldn't care less about the
dance. I've heard a bunch of guys saying
there's no way they're gonna pay three bucks
to go to a dance in the school gymnasium.
But that all changed earlier this week when
the first Candy Grams got handed out in
homeroom.

The Candy Grams are invitations to the Valentine's Day dance, and the Dance Committee started selling them at lunch the other day. If you pay twenty-five cents, you can send a Candy Gram to anyone you want, and Bryce Anderson got ones from at least five different girls right off the bat.

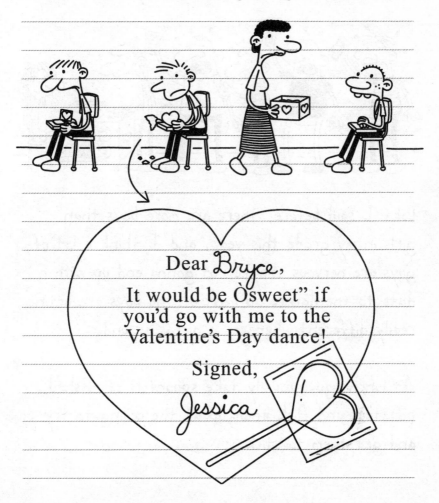

Dear Bryce,
It would be "sweet" if you'd go with me to the Valentine's Day dance!
Signed,
Jessica

After the first wave of Candy Grams got delivered, some of the boys who didn't get one got jealous of the guys who DID. Now all of a sudden EVERYONE wants to go to the dance because no one wants to be left out. So yesterday at lunch there was a big rush on Candy Grams.

Like I said before, there are more boys than girls in my grade this year, and I think a lot of guys are nervous they're not gonna end up with a date to the dance. So most of the boys are acting really different whenever a girl is around.

At lunch, guys usually take spoonfuls of mashed potatoes and flick them up at the ceiling to try and get them to stick.

Don't even ask me WHAT they put in the potatoes that makes them stick like that.

Sometimes I forget to look up before I find a place to sit.

The girls really hate the mashed potato thing, and that's why they sit on the other side of the cafeteria. But now the boys know they're not gonna get one of the girls to go with them to the dance if they act like jerks.

I can tell it's hard for a lot of the boys to be mature in front of the girls. So some guys are acting out when there aren't any girls around.

We're in the middle of a basketball unit in Phys Ed, with the girls playing on one side of the gym and the boys on the other. The other day this kid named Anthony Renfrew thought it would be pretty funny if he pantsed Daniel Revis when he was shooting free throws.

Everybody laughed except for Daniel, but later on Daniel got Anthony back when he was going for a layup. After that it was a free-for-all, with everyone pantsing everyone else. So things have been AWFUL since then.

Now everyone's so paranoid about getting pantsed that no one will even stand up during our basketball scrimmages.

I've even started wearing two pairs of shorts under my sweatpants for extra insurance.

Things have gotten so bad that Vice Principal Roy came into the gym today to lecture the boys. He said this was no laughing matter and that anyone caught pantsing another student would be suspended.

But Vice Principal Roy should've watched where he was standing, because some kid snuck under the bleachers and got him pretty good.

Whoever did it escaped before Vice Principal Roy could catch him. No one knows for sure who it was, but the name they're using for the guy is the Mad Pantser.

Tuesday
It's been about a week since they introduced these Candy Grams, and I'm getting a little concerned that I haven't gotten one yet. I've never flung potatoes on the ceiling and I've never pantsed anyone in my life, so I don't know what a guy needs to do to impress a girl these days.

It seems like every guy in my homeroom has gotten a Candy Gram. Even Travis Hickey got one, and he'll eat a crust of pizza out of a trash can if you give him a quarter.

Uncle Gary was playing his computer game in my room the other night, and I told him about the Valentine's Day dance and the Candy Grams. Believe it or not, he gave me some really good advice.

Uncle Gary told me the best way to get a girl's attention is by making yourself look "unavailable." He said what I should do is buy a bunch of Candy Grams and have them all delivered to MYSELF so the girls would think I was a really hot property.

I probably should've thought about talking to Uncle Gary a lot earlier. He's been married something like four times already, so he's an EXPERT on relationships.

Yesterday I bought two dollars' worth of Candy Grams, and today in homeroom they were delivered to me.

HERE'S ANOTHER ONE FOR GREG HEFFLEY!

YAWN!

I just hope this works, because that two bucks was my lunch money.

Friday

By Wednesday I'd blown through five dollars, and I realized if I kept buying Candy Grams for myself, I was gonna starve to death. So I decided to actually buy a Candy Gram for a GIRL and see how that went.

Yesterday at lunch I bought a Candy Gram and sent it to Adrianne Simpson, who sits three rows away from me in English. But I didn't want to risk my whole quarter on one person, so I made sure I got my money's worth.

Dear Adrianne,

It would be "sweet" if you'd go with me to the Valentine's Day dance!

Signed,
Greg Heffley

P.S. If the answer is no, please hand this to Julia Barros, who is two seats to your left.

Adrianne and Julia were both giving me dirty looks when I walked into class today, so I'm assuming it's a no from both of them.

I realized a Candy Gram isn't the ONLY way to ask a girl to a dance, though. There's a girl named Leighann Marlow who sits in the same chair for homeroom that I sit in for History class. So I wrote her a note on my desk, and it didn't cost me a cent.

Unfortunately, I forgot that after-school detention is held in the same room as History, so some moron jumped in with an answer before Leighann even had a chance to read my note.

Hi Leighann-
If you are looking for someone to go to the dance with, just let me know by writing back.

Greg Heffley

Hi Greg - I am sorry but I'm not interested in going to the dance with you.
Leighann

Dear Greg
Yes I will go to the dance with you and P.S. will you marry me?

HAR HAR HAR

KISS KISS

I'm pretty nervous, because it seems like there aren't really a lot of girls left to choose from at this point.

One girl who doesn't have a date yet is Erika Hernandez. She just broke up with her boyfriend, this kid named Jamar Law, who is famous in our school for getting his head stuck in a chair. The janitor even had to cut him free with a hacksaw. It's in the yearbook and everything.

Sticky situation: Jamar Law gets a little help from Mr. Lewis after getting his head stuck in a chair during Mrs. Moran's art class.

Erika is really pretty and nice, so don't ask me what she was thinking when she started going out with a doofus like Jamar.

She WOULD be at the top of my list for the dance. But I'm worried that if things worked out between me and her, I'd always be thinking about her ex-boyfriend and I wouldn't be able to get past it.

The Erika Hernandez situation has made me wonder what other girls might have a Jamar Law in their past. It's hard to keep track of who has gone out with who in my school, and that's important information when you're looking for a date to the dance. So I drew up a chart to see how everyone in my grade is connected.

I've still got a long way to go, but here's the incomplete version.

The person I'm worried about is a boy named Evan Whitehead. I've heard him bragging that he's kissed a bunch of different girls in my grade.

But last week he got sent home from school because he had the chicken pox, which I didn't even know you could still GET anymore. So who knows HOW many girls Evan's infected.

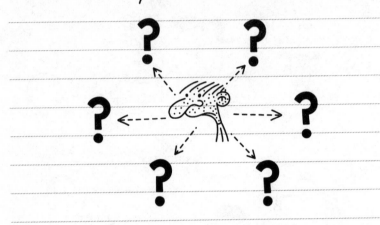

One girl I'm pretty sure Evan never kissed is Julie Webber, because she's been going out with Ed Norwell since the fifth grade. But I've heard their relationship is a little shaky these days, so I'm gonna do what I can to help speed things along.

YOU CAN DO BETTER THAN HIM!

Tuesday

Uncle Gary told me that if I want a girl to go to the dance with me, I'm gonna have to ask her face-to-face. I've been trying to avoid that, but I think he's probably right.

There's a girl named Peyton Ellis who I've always kind of had a crush on, and when I saw her drinking from the water fountain yesterday, I stood there and waited patiently for her to finish. But Peyton must've seen me out of the corner of her eye and realized I was gonna ask her to the dance, so she just kept drinking and drinking while I stood there like a dope.

Eventually, the bell rang and we both had to go to class.

I barely know Peyton, so maybe it was a bad idea
to try and ask her anyway. I realized I should
probably stick with girls who I've got some kind of
a connection with. The first person to come to mind
was Bethany Breen, my lab partner in Science.

But I don't think I've made such a good
impression on Bethany. We're in the middle of our
anatomy unit, and for the past few days we've
been dissecting frogs. I'm really squeamish when
it comes to that sort of thing, so I just let
Bethany do the dissecting while I stand on the
other side of the room trying not to throw up.

Seriously, though, in this day and age I don't
know why we're still cutting open frogs to see
what's inside them.

If somebody tells me there's a heart and intestines inside a frog, I'm willing to take their word for it.

I was pretty happy I got paired up with Bethany as lab partners. I remember back in elementary school, whenever a teacher picked a boy and a girl to do something together, all the other kids would go CRAZY.

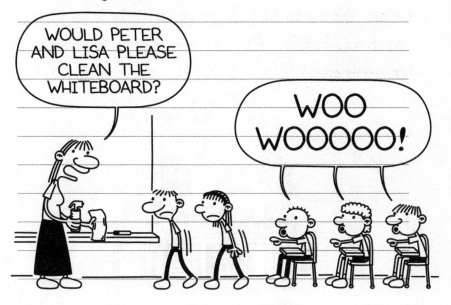

When I got picked to be lab partners with Bethany, I was hoping for some kind of reaction from the rest of the class. But I guess everyone's outgrown that stuff.

Even though I haven't impressed Bethany with my dissection skills, I still thought I might have a shot with her. I don't want to brag or anything, but I HAVE been a pretty hilarious lab partner.

At the end of the day yesterday, I walked up to Bethany when she was getting her coat out of her locker.

I admit I was a little nervous talking to her even though we spend forty-five minutes every day as lab partners. But before I got a single word out, I started thinking about the frogs. So I don't think it's gonna work out between me and her.

Last night when I was telling Uncle Gary about what happened at school, he said my problem is that I'm trying to do this on my own and I need a "wingman" to help me look good in front of the girls so it's easier to ask one out.

Well, I think Rowley would be a PERFECT wingman for me, because he makes me look good just by being himself.

Today I asked Rowley to be my wingman, but he didn't really understand the concept. So I told him it's just like being my campaign manager, but for the dance.

Rowley said maybe we could be EACH OTHER's wingman and help each other get a date to the dance, but I said we should do this one person at a time. I feel like we need to get my situation taken care of first, because getting Rowley a date to the dance could end up being a long-term project.

We gave the wingman thing a trial run at lunch, but I think there's still a lot of room for improvement.

Thursday

On the walk home from school today, Rowley told me he heard from a girl on the Dance Committee that Alyssa Grove just broke up with her boyfriend and is looking for a date to the dance.

See, that's EXACTLY why I made Rowley my wingman. Alyssa is one of the most popular girls in my school, so I was gonna have to act quick before one of the other goobers in my class got to her.

When I got home I called Alyssa's number right away, but no one was there. The answering machine picked up really fast, and the next thing I knew I was leaving a message.

I hit the "pound" key on the phone so I could delete my message and start over. But my second message wasn't that great, either.

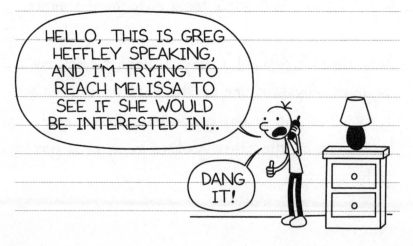

I must've recorded twenty messages, because I wanted to get it just right. But Rowley was in the room with me trying to stay completely silent, and whenever I looked at him I just completely lost it.

After a while me and Rowley were just totally having fun and goofing around.

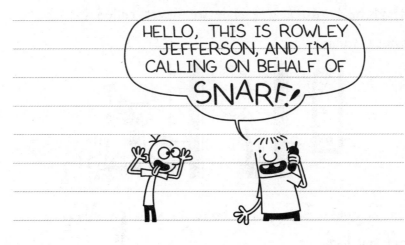

I knew there was no way I could leave a serious message while Rowley was at my house, so I deleted the last one and hung up the phone. I figured I might as well just wait until tomorrow morning and talk to Alyssa in person.

But what I didn't know was that hitting the "pound" key didn't delete my messages on the Groves' voice mail system the way it does on ours. So after dinner tonight there was a knock on the door, and it was Alyssa's father.

Mr. Grove told Dad that me and my friend had left twenty prank messages on his machine and that he'd appreciate it if we never called his house again.

So I guess I'm gonna have to scratch Alyssa off my list.

<u>Monday</u>

Uncle Gary told me if I really want to send the right signals to girls at school, I might consider updating my wardrobe. He said that wearing a new shirt or new shoes always makes him feel more confident, and it might work for me, too.

The thing is, I really don't HAVE a lot of new clothes. I'd say about 90% of everything I wear is a hand-me-down from Rodrick. Mom would say that's an exaggeration, but all you have to do is check the tags in my underwear for proof.

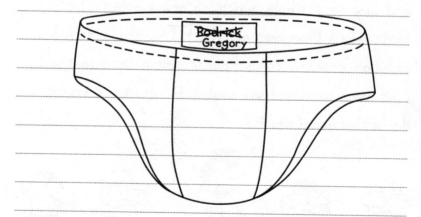

I never really cared much about what I wore, but now Uncle Gary has me wondering if my wardrobe is holding me back.

This weekend I asked Mom if we could go out and get me some new jeans and shoes so I could really look sharp at school, but the minute I said it I wished I could take it back.

Mom gave me a long speech about how kids in middle school focus too much on appearances, and how if we spent half the time on academics that we do on deciding what to wear, our country wouldn't be ranked twenty-fifth in the world in math.

I should've known Mom wouldn't run right out and buy me a whole bunch of new clothes. In fact, when Mom was on the PTA, she started a petition pushing for school uniforms because she'd read some article that said kids who wear uniforms do better in academics.

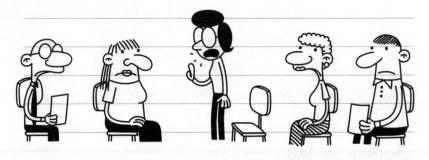

Luckily, she didn't get enough signatures, but word got around that my mom was the one who started the school uniform petition, and there was a stretch of a few weeks where I had to wait a half hour at the end of each day before it was safe to walk home.

Since Mom wouldn't take me out clothes shopping, I decided to start poking around the house to see if there was anything cool I could wear.

I started by going through Rodrick's dresser drawers, but I don't think we have the same taste when it comes to clothes.

Uncle Gary told me I should look in Dad's closet, because sometimes grown-ups have "vintage" stuff that looks cool. I've never seen Dad wear anything cool in my whole life, but I was willing to give it a try.

I'm glad Uncle Gary gave me that tip, because believe it or not, I found EXACTLY what I was looking for in the back of Dad's closet.

It was a BLACK LEATHER JACKET. I've never seen Dad wear it, so I figured he must've bought it before I was born.

I had no idea Dad owned anything that cool, and it kind of made me see him in a whole new light.

I put it on and went downstairs. Dad seemed pretty surprised to see his old leather jacket, and he said he bought it back when he was first dating Mom.

I asked Dad if I could borrow it, and he said he didn't need it anymore so it was OK by him.

Unfortunately, Mom wasn't on board with the idea. She said the jacket was way too expensive for a middle school student to wear and that I might damage it or lose it.

I told her that wasn't fair, because it was just sitting in the closet gathering dust, so it didn't really matter if something happened to it. But Mom said the jacket sent the "wrong message" and that, besides, it wasn't a winter coat. So she told me to put it back in the upstairs closet.

But when I was in the shower this morning, I just couldn't stop thinking about how awesome it would be to wear that thing to school. I knew I could probably sneak it out of the house and put it back in the closet later without Mom even noticing.

So while she was feeding Manny breakfast, I went upstairs, grabbed the jacket, and slipped out the front door.

The first thing I have to say is, Mom was right about the jacket not being a winter coat.

That thing didn't have any sort of lining, and halfway to school I was starting to really regret my decision.

My gloves were in my winter coat at home, and my hands were FREEZING. So I shoved them in the pockets of the jacket, but there was something in each one.

There was a really cool pair of aviator sunglasses in one of the pockets, so that was a bonus. In the other there was one of those picture strips you get at a photo booth in the mall.

At first I didn't recognize the people in the
picture, but then I realized it was Mom and Dad.

I really wish I hadn't seen that right after
eating breakfast.

When I got to school, every head turned in my
direction as I walked down the hallway.

In fact, I got so much attention that I
decided to keep the jacket on the rest of the
day. I felt like a whole new person in homeroom.

A few minutes before the bell rang to start the
day, there was a loud knocking on the little
window in the door.

I just about had a heart attack when I saw who it was.

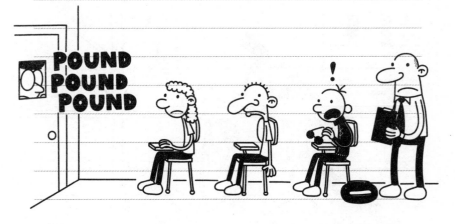

When the teacher opened the door, Mom walked straight to my desk and made me hand over Dad's leather jacket in front of everyone.

I told Mom it was too cold outside for me to walk home without a jacket, so she gave me HER winter coat to wear.

I wasn't too happy about the situation, but at least I was warm on the way home.

Wednesday

By now everybody at school has heard about the guy whose Mom made him wear her winter coat. So this is gonna make it a lot harder for me to find a date to the dance.

That's why I've decided my best shot is to take someone who DOESN'T go to my school to the dance. And I think I've found the perfect place to look: church.

I've heard that the students at the church school think the kids who go to public school are pretty tough. So whenever I run into one of my friends at church, I make sure to play it real cool in front of the church kids.

Recently, Mom has become friends with Mrs. Stringer at church because they both worked on the Fall Fair Committee.

The Stringers have two kids who go to the church
school, a boy named Wesley and a girl named
Laurel. I've never actually seen Wesley, so he must
be down in the basement with the other little kids
during church.

MR.   LAUREL   MRS.
STRINGER STRINGER   STRINGER

A few nights ago Mom invited the whole Stringer
family over to our house for dinner this Friday.
I think she's hoping Manny and Wesley will click
and Manny can be friends with a real live person
for once.

But I can see a real opportunity here for ME.
Laurel is in my grade, and she's better looking
than most of the girls in my class. So this dinner
could really change my fortunes.

Friday

Mom spent a long time getting the house ready before the Stringers came over, and when I took a look around, I realized I'd better pitch in, too.

There were embarrassing things all over the place. For starters, we still had our Christmas tree up in the living room. It was too much work to dismantle it, so me and Dad just shoved it in the garage.

DOINK

There were diapers taped on all the corners of our family room furniture that were left over from when Mom baby-proofed the house after Manny started crawling.

She used packing tape to hold the diapers in place, and THAT wasn't easy to get off.

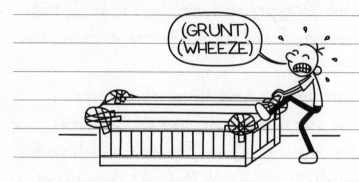

Uncle Gary was on the couch in the family room taking a nap, so we just covered him with a sheet and hoped nobody would want to sit there.

Next was the kitchen. There's a bulletin board on the wall with different certificates and ribbons that Mom has given us kids over the years.

Everything with my name on it is really lame, so I took it off the wall and hid it in the pantry.

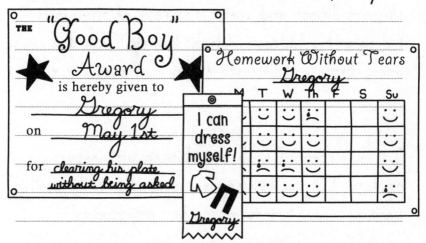

By the time the Stringers showed up, we'd taken care of all the major stuff. But the visit got off to a really shaky start. You remember how I said Manny was afraid of some kid at church who acted like a vampire? Well, it turns out that kid was Wesley Stringer.

So any hope Mom had of Manny making a new friend was completely out the window. Manny skipped dinner and spent the rest of the night hiding in his bedroom, which I wish I could've done, because Mom made a fancy meal to impress our guests.

It was cream of mushroom chicken with asparagus on top. I know asparagus is supposed to be really good for you, but to me it's like kryptonite.

I didn't want to look unsophisticated in front of Laurel, though, so I decided to just close my eyes, plug my nose, and choke it down.

The grown-ups talked about politics and stuff that wasn't all that interesting, and me and Laurel just had to sit there and listen.

Mom told Mrs. Stringer about some fancy restaurant she goes to with Dad when they have a "date night," and Mrs. Stringer said that she and her husband can never go out for dinner on weekends because Laurel is always off doing something with friends and they can't find a reliable babysitter for Wesley.

I told Mrs. Stringer that if they ever need a babysitter, they should call ME.

I figured it's a way to get in good with the Stringers and get paid doing it. Mom liked the idea, too, and she said babysitting would be a great experience for me. Mrs. Stringer seemed pretty impressed, and she asked if I was free tomorrow, so I told her I was.

I don't want to get too far ahead of myself here, but I'm sure one day I'll be sitting around with the Stringers on Thanksgiving and we'll all be laughing about how I used to babysit my brother-in-law, Wesley, when I was in middle school.

Saturday
Tonight Mom dropped me off at the Stringers' house at 6:30.

Mrs. Stringer said Laurel had already gone to a friend's house, which kind of stunk, because I was hoping I might get to see her for a few minutes and talk to her about the dance.

Mrs. Stringer said I should put Wesley to bed at 8:00 and that they'd be home around 9:00. She told me I could watch TV until they got home and to help myself to anything in the fridge.

After Mr. and Mrs. Stringer left, it was just me and Wesley. I asked Wesley if he wanted to play a board game or something like that, but he said he wanted to go out in the garage and get his bike.

I told him it was too cold to ride his bike outside, but he said he wanted to ride it INSIDE. The Stringers have a really nice house, and I was pretty sure they didn't want Wesley scratching up their hardwood floors. So I told him we needed to find something else to do.

Wesley had a huge fit. After he calmed down he told me he wanted to color instead. I asked him where his coloring stuff was, and he said it was in the laundry room. But when I went to get it, I heard the latch on the door lock behind me.

Then I heard the garage door open, and the next thing I knew Wesley was riding around the kitchen on his bike.

I pounded on the door for him to let me out, but he just ignored me.

Next I heard the basement door open, and then a rumbling sound followed by a HUGE crash. I could hear Wesley crying at the bottom of the stairs, and I started to panic because it sounded like he was really hurt.

But then Wesley calmed down, and I could hear him dragging his bike back up to the top of the stairs. Then he rode down the stairs and crashed at the bottom AGAIN, followed by MORE tears.

I am not exaggerating when I tell you this went on for an hour and a half. I thought Wesley would wear himself out, but he never did. I remembered that the Stringers said they couldn't find a babysitter for Wesley, and now that was starting to make a lot of sense.

I figured I was gonna have to punish Wesley for locking me in the laundry room once I got out of there. What he DESERVED was a good spanking, but I figured that probably wouldn't fly with the Stringers.

I decided I'd give Wesley a time-out, because that's what my parents always did when I misbehaved as a little kid. In fact, when I was little I even got time-outs from RODRICK.

The thing is, I had no idea Rodrick didn't actually have the AUTHORITY to give me time-outs. And I can't tell you how many hours I logged in that time-out chair when Rodrick was babysitting me.

One time I was throwing a ball in the house while I was home alone with Rodrick, and I accidentally knocked over a wedding photo of Mom and Dad. Rodrick gave me a half-hour time-out for THAT one.

When Mom and Dad got home, they saw the broken picture and asked which one of us had done it. I told them it was me but that they didn't need to give me a punishment, because I'd already gotten a time-out from RODRICK.

But Mom said the only people who could hand out punishments were her and Dad, so I ended up serving a DOUBLE time-out for breaking that picture.

BRUSH
BRUSH

I figured Wesley deserved a TRIPLE time-out for locking me in the laundry room. But it was getting pretty late, and I knew it would look bad if the Stringers came home and I was still locked inside.

So I started looking for another way out. There was a spare freezer blocking a door to the back deck, so I pushed with all my might and gave myself just enough room to squeeze through and open the door.

It was really cold outside, and I was only wearing a T-shirt and pants. I tried to open the front door, but it was locked.

I decided if I was gonna catch this kid off guard, I'd need the element of surprise. So I walked around the house and tried all the windows on the first floor until I found one that was unlocked. I then pushed it open and crawled inside.

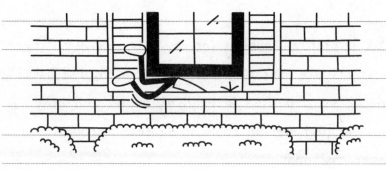

I landed headfirst in someone's bedroom, and after
I looked around I realized it must be Laurel's.

Like I said, it was freezing cold outside, so I
needed to warm up before going after Wesley. But
I really regret taking a few minutes to do that,
because in the time I was in Laurel's room, Mr.
and Mrs. Stringer came home.

AAAHHH...

Hopefully, we can all have a good chuckle about this story at some future Thanksgiving, too. But I think it's gonna be a while before Mr. Stringer is ready to laugh about this one.

Wednesday

After blowing my chances with Laurel Stringer, I pretty much gave up on finding someone to take to the dance. It's only three days away, and by now everyone who's going is already paired up with someone else. So I figured I'd be spending Saturday night at home playing video games by myself.

But yesterday Rowley gave me some news after one of his Dance Committee meetings that changed EVERYTHING.

He said Abigail Brown was upset during the meeting because the boy she was going with, Michael Sampson, has a family obligation and had to cancel on her. So now Abigail has a dress and no one to go to the dance with.

So the stage is set for me to swoop in and be the hero. I told Rowley this was his big chance to come through as my wingman and hook me up with Abigail.

The thing is, Abigail doesn't really know me, and I kind of doubted she'd go to the dance with a person she doesn't know. So I told Rowley he should tell Abigail the three of us could go to the dance TOGETHER as a "group of friends."

Rowley seemed to like that idea because he's been doing all this work on the Dance Committee and didn't have anyone to go with, either.

I figured the three of us could go out to dinner, and at the restaurant Abigail would get to see what a great guy I was. By the time we got to the dance, we'd walk in as a couple.

The only problem was that we'd need a RIDE. I wasn't about to ask Mom for one, because the seats in our minivan are crusted with old Cheerios and God knows what else. Plus, having Mom along on my date could be a total disaster.

IT SEEMS LIKE IT WAS JUST YESTERDAY THAT GREG WAS IN DIAPERS!

I knew if I really wanted to impress Abigail, I'd need to rent a limo, but those things cost a FORTUNE. Then I had an idea.

Rowley's dad has a really nice car, so I figured we could get HIM to drive us. Abigail wouldn't even have to know Mr. Jefferson was Rowley's dad. If we didn't say anything, she'd just think he was a professional driver. Maybe I'll even get him one of those hats chauffeurs wear, to really sell the idea.

Of course, we wouldn't be able to say anything to MR. JEFFERSON, either. Me and him kind of have a bad history, and I'm sure he wouldn't be looking to do me any extra favors.

Things started falling into place today. Rowley talked to Abigail, and she likes the whole "group of friends" idea. And on top of that, Mr. Jefferson agreed to drive us to the dance.

So now I'm keeping my fingers crossed that nothing will happen between now and Saturday night to screw things up.

Friday
I told Uncle Gary about the dance, and he seems even more excited about it than I am. He wanted to know all the details, like how many people were gonna be there and if they hired a DJ. But I didn't know the answers to his questions, because Rowley's the one on the Dance Committee and that stuff is kind of in his department.

I was more focused on finding something to WEAR. Uncle Gary told me if I really want to impress my date, I should wear a suit. I went in Rodrick's closet and found a suit that he actually wore to one of Uncle Gary's weddings.

I couldn't find any cologne in Rodrick's junk drawer, but I DID find a bottle of that body spray they're always advertising on TV. I was a little nervous about using it, though, because if that stuff really works like they say in the ads, then tomorrow night could be a nightmare.

SCREAAAAAMM!!!

My Great Uncle Bruce passed away a few years ago, and I knew we had a box with some of his personal stuff in the garage. I found a bottle of his cologne and tried a little on my wrist.

It made me smell exactly like Great Uncle Bruce, but I figure it's safer than using that body spray.

I even asked Dad to take me to the grocery store, where I bought a box of those Valentine's chocolates for Abigail. I never should've taken the cellophane off the box, though, because I've already helped myself to the buttercreams, peanut clusters, and caramels.

Hopefully, Abigail likes the coconut chocolates and the ones that taste like toothpaste, because that's all that's really left at this point.

Saturday
Tonight was the night of the big Valentine's Day dance, and it got off to a REALLY rough start.

When I went over to Rowley's house to get ready, I noticed he had little red bumps on his face that looked like mosquito bites. But then I realized what those spots were: CHICKEN POX.

Ever since Evan Whitehead showed up at school with chicken pox a few weeks ago, it's been spreading like wildfire in my class.

This past week four boys were sent home by the school nurse. I'm pretty sure one of those guys was the Mad Pantser, because there haven't been any pantsing incidents since Tuesday.

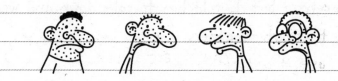

I've heard chicken pox are SUPER contagious, and whenever a kid gets them, they're not allowed to come back to school for a week. But I couldn't afford to have Rowley out of commission for even one NIGHT. He was my ride to the dance, and I knew that if his mom and dad didn't let him go, then I couldn't go, either.

I told Rowley he had the chicken pox, but I probably should've broken the news to him slowly instead of all at once.

Rowley was gonna go straight downstairs and tell his parents, but I told him to calm down and we'd figure this out together.

I said if he could just get through the night without telling anyone, I'd owe him for the rest of my life. All he needed to do was cover up his chicken pox and not make a big stink to his parents. We'd both go to the dance and have a great time, and no one would even have to know.

But Rowley was too freaked out to think straight, and I had to give him two coconut chocolates to quiet him down.

Now that Rowley knew he had the chicken pox, he was going CRAZY with the itching. So I got some socks out of his dresser and put them on his hands.

I figured Rowley's mom and dad probably knew
what chicken pox looked like and we had to find
a way to cover them up. So we went into his
parents' bathroom and looked through his Mom's
makeup kit to see if there was anything we could
use. I found some stuff called "concealer," and
that sounded about right to me.

I used a little brush I found in a drawer and
then tried to cover up the problem areas on
Rowley's face.

But you could totally tell that Rowley was wearing
makeup. So I grabbed a silk scarf from the
top of Mrs. Jefferson's dresser and told Rowley
to put it on and cover up around his mouth.
Then I noticed he had a few chicken pox on his
FOREHEAD, so I found a beach hat in his mom's
closet and had him put that on, too.

I'm not gonna say Rowley looked totally normal, but at least you couldn't tell he had the chicken pox.

I kind of held my breath when we got into the car, but I think Mr. Jefferson just thought Rowley's getup was some kind of middle school fashion thing, and he didn't say a word.

When I opened the back door to get in, I was pretty surprised to find Rowley's old booster seat taking up one of the spots.

I asked Rowley why he still had a booster seat in his dad's car, and he said they just never took it out once he got big enough for the regular seat. But come to think of it, I've always thought Rowley seemed a little too tall whenever he drove by with his family.

I knew we had to take that thing out before we went to pick up Abigail, because a limo company would never have a booster seat in one of its cars.

But you needed to be some kind of an engineer to figure out how to undo the clasp on that thing. By that point we were already late picking up Abigail, so we had to just leave it.

When we pulled into Abigail's driveway, I asked Mr. Jefferson to honk the horn to let her know we were there.

But Mr. Jefferson wouldn't honk the horn, because he said that's no way to treat a "lady." He said one of us was gonna have to go to her front door and "escort" her.

Rowley started to get out, but I realized this was my big chance to make a good first impression on Abigail. So I walked up to the house and knocked on the door.

But Abigail didn't come to the front door—her DAD did. Apparently, Mr. Brown is a state trooper, or he just likes dressing up like one.

Mr. Brown said Abigail was upstairs getting ready and she'd be down in a minute.

He told me to come inside and have a seat while I waited. It felt like we were sitting there an HOUR waiting for Abigail to come downstairs, and I really didn't like the look of the handcuffs Mr. Brown had on his belt.

I finally decided this was way too much stress for a Valentine's Day dance and was ready to bail out. But right as I went to leave, Abigail came down the stairs.

The first thing I noticed was that Abigail was wearing a really poofy dress, and I knew there was no way the three of us were gonna fit in the backseat of Mr. Jefferson's car. But there was no way I was sitting in Rowley's booster seat, either, so I volunteered to ride up front. Besides, I knew Mr. Jefferson had heated front seats, so I figured I might as well take advantage of that.

Mr. Jefferson had a pile of papers in the passenger seat because I guess he was planning on doing his taxes or something while he was waiting for us at the dance.

It was too much of a hassle to move all that stuff, so I decided to just hop in the way back of the car so we could get on with the night.

Abigail didn't seem too bothered by the fact that Rowley was sitting in a booster seat, and I'm pretty sure she thought he was just doing it as a joke.

But humor is kind of MY thing, and I wasn't about to let Rowley steal my thunder.

It got kind of quiet in the car, so I asked Mr. Jefferson if he could turn on the radio. But instead of putting on some music, he tuned in to some boring talk radio station, and that's what we had to listen to for the rest of the ride.

I'm pretty sure he just did that because he was annoyed I'd called him "Driver."

Rowley and Abigail got into a conversation, but I was right next to the speakers in the back and I couldn't really hear what they were saying.

When Mr. Jefferson pulled over, I thought we were at the restaurant. But we'd stopped at a repair shop to pick up Mr. Jefferson's vacuum cleaner.

At that point I wished I'd just coughed up the money for a limo, because a professional driver wouldn't have run errands on the way to the restaurant.

I'd made a reservation at Spriggo's, which is that fancy restaurant Mom and Dad are always talking about. I knew it might be a little pricey, but I'd saved up a lot of money from chores and I really wanted to impress Abigail by looking like a big shot.

When we pulled into the parking lot, Mr. Jefferson opened the back for me. But when I got out, my suit was covered in all these greasy smears from the vacuum cleaner.

I didn't want to look like a slob, so I just left my jacket in the car, and we went into the restaurant together. I was hoping Rowley would take a hint and stay back with his dad, but he came right along with us.

Spriggo's

Spriggo's was a LOT fancier than I thought it would be. When we walked in, the host told us this was an "upscale establishment" and that gentlemen were required to wear sports jackets.

But there was no way I was gonna wear my dirty suit jacket, so I asked the host if he could just make an exception this one time. He said he couldn't but that the restaurant had spare sports jackets I could borrow. The one he gave me was a little big, but I put it on anyway.

When we sat down I noticed a terrible smell and tried to figure out where it was coming from. Then I realized it was coming from ME. I guess that loaner jacket had been used by a hundred different people without ever being washed.

I didn't want to smell like somebody else's body odor during dinner, so I excused myself to go to the bathroom and scrubbed the sports jacket's underarms with soap and water, then dried them with the hand dryer.

Well, that just made it WORSE, because the heat activated the B.O. and it spread.

That was it for me. I told Abigail and Rowley this place was for phonies and we should just take off.

I left my jacket with the host at the front, and the three of us walked out the door. I said maybe we should just skip dinner and go right to the dance, but Abigail said she was really hungry, and Rowley said HE was starving, too.

The only other restaurant in the area was Corny's, and I told them there was no way I was going THERE. But Rowley said he really likes the dessert bar at Corny's, and Abigail said that sounded good to her.

I was really starting to regret having Rowley along on this date, because if all he was gonna do was take Abigail's side, I'd get outvoted every single time. But I didn't want to make a big deal about it in the middle of my date, so I just bit my lip and we walked three blocks to Corny's.

Luckily, I remembered about the tie issue before we walked in the front door, and I stuffed mine in my back pocket at the last second.

But I didn't have time to warn Rowley, so now his tie is a permanent part of the Wall of Shame.

Corny's was a total ZOO. My family usually goes on a weeknight, but it's a whole different scene on a Saturday.

The good news was that since we didn't have any little kids with us, they didn't seat us in Children's Alley. But the "adult" section of Corny's wasn't a whole lot better. All that separates the two sides is some glass, and we got seated right next to a family with a bunch of wild kids.

I asked our waitress if we could move, and she made a sour face and took our stuff to another table. But I wish we had just stayed where we were, because our new situation wasn't an improvement.

I didn't want to ask the waitress to move us a SECOND time, because the last person you want to make mad is the person who's serving you your food. So I put a couple of menus up against the window to block my view.

Our waitress brought us corn chips, and Rowley took the socks off his hands so he could eat. I didn't think it was such a great idea for all of us to be grabbing chips out of the same basket while Rowley had the chicken pox, so I kept it near me.

Every time Rowley looked like he wanted a chip, I pushed one to him with a straw.

SLIDE

I couldn't remember if the chicken pox is airborne, so whenever Rowley talked I held my breath just to be sure.

At one point he told us a really long story about something that happened to him last summer, and by the end I almost passed out.

I told Abigail and Rowley that I was paying for dinner so they should get whatever they wanted. I was trying to show off a little for Abigail by throwing my money around.

But when the waitress came back, Abigail ordered TWO appetizers, and so did Rowley.

The waitress couldn't understand what Rowley was saying because of his scarf, though, and he pulled it down to speak. But when he did, a single molecule of spit flew in the air and landed on my bottom lip.

I let my jaw go totally slack so the molecule wouldn't get into my mouth. I tried to stay calm on the outside, but on the inside I was totally freaking out.

I wanted to wipe my lip with my napkin, but I'd dropped it on the floor and couldn't reach it. So I waited until Abigail was distracted and then wiped my lip on her sleeve.

We placed our order, and I asked for a plain hamburger to save money. Abigail ordered the T-bone steak, which is the most expensive item on the menu, and Rowley got the same thing even though I was trying to signal for him to order something cheap.

When our food came out, my hamburger had lettuce and tomato on it, because at Corny's they ALWAYS get your order wrong. I took off the lettuce and tomato, but there was mayonnaise on my burger, too.

When our waitress came around again, I told her I'd ordered a burger with nothing on it. So she took a napkin and just wiped the mayonnaise off, then left the napkin right in the middle of the table.

I lost my appetite after that. But even if I WAS hungry, I probably wouldn't have finished my meal anyway. If you clean your plate at Corny's, there's a picture at the bottom that I really can't stand.

I just sat there and waited while Abigail and
Rowley ate their steaks, and when they finished
I signaled for the waitress to come over so I
could pay the bill.

But then Rowley and Abigail said they wanted
dessert. The whole reason we came to Corny's in
the first place was for the dessert bar, which
comes free with your meal. But of course Rowley
and Abigail each wanted to order a SPECIAL
dessert off the menu, which costs extra.

I got up and found our waitress to tell her it was Rowley's birthday, because I knew then he'd get a free dessert. So a few minutes later the waiters and waitresses all came out and sang "Happy Birthday" to Rowley and gave him his free cake.

♪ HAPPY BIRTHDAY TO YOU, ♪
♪ HAPPY BIRTHDAY TO YOU ♪

Abigail still ordered a triple-layer chocolate cheesecake, which she only took two bites out of.

When the bill came, I couldn't BELIEVE how much it was. I had to use all the money in my wallet, and I even had to pull out the five dollars I was keeping in my sock in case of an emergency.

The waitress wouldn't take the money I had in my sock because it was a little wet, so I had to go out to the car and ask Mr. Jefferson if he had a five-dollar bill he could trade.

When I got back to the table, Rowley and Abigail were in the middle of a conversation, and it seemed to me like they were sitting a little closer than when I'd left.

182

I thought about giving Abigail a heads-up that she might want to keep her distance from Rowley, but I was afraid she'd bail on the date if she found out about the chicken pox.

The three of us got back in the car, and Mr. Jefferson drove us to school and dropped us off at the front door. He gave Rowley a big hug, which I'm sure seemed pretty weird to Abigail if she thought he really was a professional driver.

The theme of the dance was "Midnight in Paris," and I have to admit the Dance Committee did a pretty good job. The gym was decked out to look like a street in France. There was a long table set up with punch and snacks, and there was even a chocolate fountain with strawberries for dipping.

We handed over our tickets and then got in line for photos. Each couple had their picture taken in front of a backdrop of Paris.

When it was our turn, I stood with Abigail and the photographer snapped our photo. But I wish I'd known Rowley was gonna get in the picture WITH us, because I would've just skipped it.

Midnight in Paris
Valentine's Dance

Something about the DJ looked familiar to me, and when I got closer I realized it was Uncle Gary. Don't even ask me how HE got the job.

Uncle Gary must've seen it as an opportunity to unload his T-shirts on my classmates. It was dark in the gym, so kids didn't know they were getting ripped off.

One minute Abigail was standing right next to me, and the next she was gone. I finally spotted her on the other side of the gym talking with her friends.

I walked over to them, but before I got there they all went into the girls' bathroom together.

I have no idea what it is about girls that makes them go to the bathroom in groups, but something about it happening NOW really made me nervous.

I didn't know what Abigail thought of me, but I figured she was probably telling her friends right at that moment. The boys' bathroom is right next to the girls' in the gym, so I went in there and pressed my ear to the wall.

I could hear a lot of giggling, but I couldn't really make out the conversation because of all the racket in the boys' bathroom.

I tried to get people to stop making noise, but it was no use.

It got quiet on the other side of the wall, so I walked back into the gym, and Abigail and her friends were over by the punch.

At 7:50, Uncle Gary turned up the music, and it looked like the dance was gonna get started for real. But that's when some people my Gramma's age started trickling in.

By 8:00 there must have been a hundred of them crowded around the entrance. There was some sort of commotion between one of the teachers and a few of the senior citizens, so I got closer to see what was going on.

The senior citizens claimed they'd booked the gym for a town meeting about the new Senior Center. Mrs. Sheer told them she reserved the gym for the dance two weeks ago.

But the seniors said they reserved it two MONTHS ago, and they had the paperwork to prove it. The Senior Center people said us kids were gonna have to clear out of the gym so they could have their meeting.

But then some of the girls on the Dance Committee got in on the conversation, and it looked like it was about to get ugly.

Just when it seemed like a fight was gonna break out, Mrs. Sheer suggested a compromise. She said we could put up the partition in the middle of the gym and the seniors could have their meeting on one half and us kids could have our dance on the other.

PARTITION

DANCE

SENIOR CENTER MEETING

Everybody seemed to be able to live with that
idea, and the janitor put up the partition.

Losing half of the gym was kind of a bummer, but
what killed the mood was the LIGHTS. There's
only one switch for the overhead lights in the
gym, and they had to be either all on or all off.
The senior citizens wanted them on for their
meeting, so that was the end of the "Midnight in
Paris" vibe over on our side of the gym.

The bright lights were bad for Uncle Gary, too, because now all the kids who bought shirts from him could see they'd gotten ripped off, and they started demanding their money back.

Uncle Gary tried to distract everyone by turning the music up, and a lot of people hit the dance floor.

The girls danced in a big group in the middle of the gym. Every once in a while a guy would try to dance his way into the group, but the girls had formed a kind of wall that kept the boys out. I didn't really understand that until I tried to make a move to break into the circle and got totally blocked.

One of the seniors came over to our side of the gym and complained that the music was too loud and it needed to be turned way down.

So Uncle Gary lowered the volume by about 80%, and then we could hear every word of the Senior Center meeting.

LET THE RECORD SHOW THAT MRS. FISHBURN HAS SECONDED THE MOTION TO HAVE A COFFEEMAKER IN THE KITCHENETTE.

That didn't seem to bother the girls, though. A lot of them took out their personal music players and just kept dancing.

By that point most of the boys had had enough.
All that time being on their best behavior around
the girls had taken its toll, and a lot of the guys
just totally cut loose.

Mrs. Sheer and the rest of the chaperones tried
to calm the boys down, but it was hopeless. It
was a really wild scene, and it was actually getting
a little dangerous.

I thought about going over by the bleachers to
get out of everyone's way, but at that moment
the Mad Pantser struck again and I decided I
was better off where I was.

Every once in a while, a few latecomers would walk in and turn right back around when they saw what was happening in the gym. But at around 9:00, Michael Sampson walked in holding hands with Cherie Bellanger.

Michael was the boy Abigail was SUPPOSED to go to the dance with, but I guess his "family obligation" story was just a lie.

And judging from the look on his face, I don't think he was expecting Abigail to be there, either.

After that, it was just a whole lot of drama. Michael took off and left his date behind, and Abigail spent the next half hour bawling her eyes out in the corner of the gym.

I did what I could to help make Abigail feel better, but she kind of had a crowd around her, so I'm not sure she actually noticed.

Right about that time, the Senior Center meeting wrapped up, and a few of the seniors started drifting over to our side of the gym and helping themselves to the refreshments.

They went through the strawberries pretty quick, and then there was nothing for people to dip in the chocolate fountain.

So kids started sticking their fingers directly in the fountain, and it was Corny's all over again.

One kid lost a contact lens in the chocolate fountain, and Mrs. Sheer had everyone stand back so she could fish it out when it cycled back through.

Since the meeting was over, Uncle Gary turned the music back up.

But the old folks started making song requests, and the next thing you knew, our Valentine's Day dance was overrun by senior citizens.

I just watched everything play out from my spot against the back wall, wondering why I'd even wanted to go to the dance in the first place. I was also starting to regret not wearing the body spray I found in Rodrick's junk drawer, because Great Uncle Bruce's cologne was attracting people outside my age group.

SNIFF
SNIFF

WAVE

It was almost 10:00, and Uncle Gary announced that the next song would be the last one of the night. When the music started playing, a few kids paired up and walked out on the dance floor as couples, which was the first time that had happened all night.

I couldn't wait for the song to end, because this dance was a total disaster, and I just wanted to go home and play some video games so I could erase the whole experience from my brain.

But just when I thought things couldn't get any worse, I saw Ruby Bird and she was coming right for me.

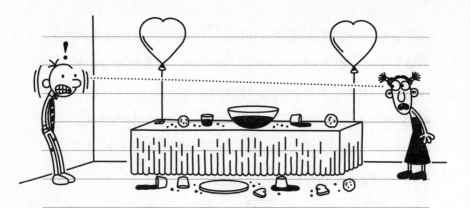

I didn't know if she was gonna ask me to dance or if I'd somehow done something to make her mad, but I did not want to end up getting bitten at a middle school dance.

I looked for some way to escape, but I was trapped. Luckily, Abigail walked right out of the bathroom at that exact moment, and I grabbed her hand just before Ruby got to me.

Abigail's makeup was a mess from all the crying, but I didn't really care. I was just happy to have an excuse to get away from Ruby. And to be honest with you, I think Abigail was happy to see me, too, so I led her to an empty spot on the dance floor.

I'd never slow-danced with a girl before, so I didn't know where I was supposed to put my hands. She put hers on my shoulders, and I put mine in my pockets, but that felt kind of dumb. So we met in the middle, and that seemed about right.

Then I noticed something on Abigail's chin. It was a little red bump that looked EXACTLY like one of Rowley's chicken pox.

Now, before I say what happened next, let me just explain in my defense that I was already on edge about the whole chicken pox thing.

But I admit, I MAY have overreacted a little.

It turns out it WASN'T chicken pox, though. It was just a pimple. When Abigail was crying, her makeup must've washed off her chin.

Anyway, I know that NOW, but anyone in my shoes probably would've reacted the same exact way I did.

But I don't think Abigail saw it that way, because on the ride home she wasn't real chatty with me.

When we pulled up to Abigail's house, Rowley walked her to the front door. That was fine with me, because it gave me a chance to finish off the rest of the chocolates. And after the night I just had, I was totally STARVING.

Wednesday
A lot has happened since the Valentine's Day dance.

A few days ago Uncle Gary bought a bunch of
scratch tickets with the money he made selling
T-shirts, and one of his tickets was a forty-
thousand-dollar winner. So he paid Dad the money
he owed him, wished me luck with the "ladies," and
moved out of the house.

The other big news is that I got a full-blown
case of the chicken pox.

I can't say for sure how I got them, but I really hope it wasn't from Rowley, because I'm not that crazy about the idea of a bunch of Rowley's virus cells attacking my immune system.

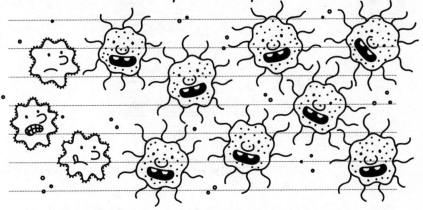

I'm pretty sure I DIDN'T get the chicken pox from Rowley, though. I've seen him walking to school the past few days, and from what I can tell, he's been wearing his mom's makeup on his chin. So I think those red bumps might've been pimples, just like Abigail's.

And speaking of Rowley and Abigail, I heard that the two of them are a couple now. All I can say is if that's true, it makes Rowley the worst wingman in history.

I'm supposed to stay home from school for at least a week. The good news is that with everyone out of the house, I can take long baths without anyone bothering me.

But I will admit all that floating around isn't as great as I remember it, and after just an hour your skin gets all wrinkly. So don't ask me how I lived that way for nine months.

Plus, I get a little lonely being by myself all day. Or at least I THINK I'm alone. Today I had a fresh towel next to the tub, and when I opened my eyes it was gone.

So either somebody's messing with me, or Johnny Cheddar is at it again.

ACKNOWLEDGMENTS

Thanks to my wonderful family for all your encouragement and for all the laughs. A lot of our stories are laced in these books, and it's been great fun to share this adventure with all of you.

Thanks to everyone at Abrams for publishing these books and for putting so much care into making them as good as they can be. Thanks to Charlie Kochman for treating every book like it's the first. Thanks to Michael Jacobs for everything you've done to make Greg Heffley reach his full potential. Thanks to Jason Wells, Veronica Wasserman, Scott Auerbach, Chad W. Beckerman, and Susan Van Metre for your dedication and for your fellowship. We've had lots of good times, and there are many more to come.

Thanks to everyone at my job—Jess Brallier and the entire team at Poptropica—for your support, camaraderie, and dedication to creating great stories for kids.

Thanks to Sylvie Rabineau, my terrific agent, for your encouragement and guidance. Thanks to Elizabeth Gabler, Carla Hacken, Nick D'Angelo, Nina Jacobson, Brad Simpson, and David Bowers for bringing Greg Heffley and his family to life on the big screen.

Thanks to Shaelyn Germain for making things run smoothly behind the scenes and for helping in so many ways.

ABOUT THE AUTHOR

Jeff Kinney is an online game developer and designer, and a #1 *New York Times* bestselling author. Jeff has been named one of *Time* magazine's 100 Most Influential People in the World. Jeff is also the creator of Poptropica.com, which was named one of *Time* magazine's 50 Best Websites. He spent his childhood in the Washington, D.C., area and moved to New England in 1995. Jeff lives in southern Massachusetts with his wife and their two sons.

杰夫·金尼 中国行

Jeff Kinney's Visit to China

2015年对中国的"哈屁族"来说，是具有划时代意义的一年！因为《小屁孩日记》的作者杰夫·金尼终于掘出了他童年梦想中的那条地道，从美国到地球另一边的中国来啦！

北京是"杰夫·金尼2015全球巡回活动"的第4站。2015年11月4日，以扁平娃斯坦利为首的一众小编终于在北京首都国际机场迎来了"小屁孩之父"杰夫·金尼！

主角登场！

接下来的11月5日，重头戏轮番上演啦！

★ 杰夫叔叔先是参加了《小屁孩日记》中文版发行600万册的庆祝会，并在会上宣布了他的新书出版计划。

大家要关注《小屁孩日记》的新书哟！

中国儿童文学作家颜值都那么高吗？（设计对白）

★ 然后，他跟中国著名儿童文学作家"阳光姐姐"伍美珍就中美少儿课外阅读情况展开了对谈。

杰夫叔叔原来也好亲切呀！（设计对白）

★ 活动现场也来了很多"哈屁族"，自然少不了签书环节，《小屁孩日记》真是大小通吃呢！

★ 不少书迷一拿到书就迫不及待地看了起来，你看，头都要扎到书里去啦！

★ 杰夫叔叔还收获了"哈屁族"送的一大堆礼物。这位小读者好有心思呀，让杰夫叔叔认识了自己的中文名。

★ 11月5日下午，杰夫叔叔还到当当网的总部接受了访谈，回答了很多有趣的问题，例如：

主持人　通过今天上午的接触，您觉得中国的小读者跟您想象的小读者是一样的吗？

我觉得全球的孩子都是一样的，他们都有父母、兄弟姐妹、有宠物和老师，所以这就是我的书为什么能受到这些孩子欢迎的原因，因为世界各地的孩子们的童年是有很多共通之处的。

主持人　因为这本书里面的事情太逼真了，会让人觉得很多事情是不是发生在您自己小时候，或者发生在您孩子的身上？

这些故事大部分其实都是有一些真人真事的依据的，然后根据这些事进行的改编。比如说我刚才随手翻开一页，这一页描述的是，格雷在院子里面找他祖母的戒指。这个故事确有其事……

篇幅有限，未能尽录。

好玩的问题还有很多呢，大家一定还想看看杰夫叔叔的回答吧？不要着急，只要关注"新世纪童书绘"的微信公众号（搜索"xsjpublish"，或扫描右手边的二维码），在对话框输入"小屁孩"并发送，就可以看到这次访谈的全部内容啦！

★ 11月5日晚上，杰夫叔叔来到北京西单图书大厦，跟广大读者见面，还给大家示范了"小屁孩"格雷的画法。

★ 活动结束后，杰夫叔叔还没能休息哦！他被带到一堆"书山"前面，这是要干什么呢？

当然是为广大读者谋福利啦！你们想要的亲笔签名本，就是从这个"深夜流水线"上扒下来的。

立刻关注全国各大书店及各大网络书店的动态，即有机会获得杰夫·金尼亲笔签名的《小屁孩日记》。

★ 11月6日，杰夫叔叔终于如愿来到了神秘又古老的故宫。

好兴奋！可以跟杰夫叔叔同游故宫耶！（设计对白）

好兴奋！终于到故宫啦！（设计对白）

又被读者逮住索要签名了。

跟扁平娃斯坦利来张合照吧！茄子！

杰夫叔叔短短两天的中国之旅就这样愉快地结束啦！你们想再见到他吗？想他到你的城市去吗？赶快关注"新世纪童书绘"的微信公众号（搜索"xsjpublish"，或扫描前页的二维码）和"小屁孩日记官方微博"（http://weibo.com/wimpywimpy），或者打电话到020-83795744，把你们的愿望告诉小编吧！

望子快乐

朱子庆

在一个人的一生中，"与有荣焉"的机会或有，但肯定不多。因为儿子译了一部畅销书，而老爸被邀涂鸦几句，像这样的与荣，我想，即使放眼天下，也没有几人领得吧。

儿子接活儿翻译《小屁孩日记》时，还在读着大三。这是安安他第一次领译书稿，多少有点紧张和兴奋吧，起初他每译几段，便"飞鸽传书"，不一会儿人也跟过来，在我面前"项庄舞剑"地问："有意思么？有意思么？"怎么当时我就没有作乐不可支状呢？于今想来，我竟很有些后悔。对于一个喂饱段子与小品的中国人，若说还有什么洋幽默能令我们"绝倒"，难！不过，安安译成杀青之时，图文并茂，我得以从头到尾再读一遍，我得当说，这部书岂止有意思呢，读了它使我有一种冲动，假如时间可以倒流，我很想尝试重新做一回父亲！我不免窃想，安安在译它的时候，不知会怎样腹诽我这个老爸呢！

我宁愿儿子是书里那个小屁孩！

你可能会说，你别是在做秀吧，小屁孩格雷将来能出息成个什么样子，实在还很难说……这个质疑，典型地出诸一个中国人之口，出之于为父母的中国人之口。望子成龙，一定要孩子出息成个什么样子，虽说初衷也是为了孩子，但最终却是苦了孩子。"生年不满百，常怀千岁忧。"现在，由于这深重的忧患，我们已经把成功学启示的模式都做到胎教了！而望子快乐，有谁想过？从小就快乐，快乐一生？惭愧，我也是看了《小屁孩日记》才想到这点，然而儿子已不再年少！我觉得很有些对不住儿子！

我从来没有对安安的"少年老成"感到过有什么不妥，毕竟少年老成使人放心。而今读其译作而被触动，此心才为之不安起来。我在想，比起美国的小屁孩格雷和他的同学们，我们中国的小屁孩们是不是活得不很小屁孩？是不是普遍地过于负重、乏乐和少年老成？而当他们将来长大，娶妻（嫁夫）生子（女），为人父母，会不会还要循此逻辑再造下一代？想想安安少年时，起早贪黑地读书、写作业，小四眼，十足一个书呆子，类似格雷那样的调皮、贪玩、小有恶搞、缰绳牢笼不住地敢于尝试和行动主义……太缺少了。印象中，安安最突出的一次，也就是读小学三年级时，做了一回带头大哥，拔了校园里所有自行车的气门芯并四处派发，仅此而已吧（此处请在家长指导下阅读）。

说点别的吧。中国作家写的儿童文学作品，很少能引发成年读者的阅读兴趣。安徒生童话之所以风靡天下，在于它征服了成年读者。在我看来，《小屁孩日记》也属于成人少年兼宜的读物，可以父子同修！谁没有年少轻狂？谁没有豆蔻年华？只不过呢，对于为父母者，阅读它，会使你由会心一笑而再笑，继以感慨系之，进而不免有所自省，对照和检讨一下自己和孩子的关系，以及在某些类似事情的处理上，自己是否欠妥？等等。它虽系成人所作，书中对孩子心性的把握，却准确传神；虽非心理学著作，对了解孩子的心理和行为，也不无参悟和启示。品学兼优和顽劣不学的孩子毕竟是少数，小屁孩格雷是"中间人物"的一个玲珑典型，着实招人怜爱——在格雷身上，有着我们彼此都难免有的各样小心思、小算计、小毛病，就好像阿Q，读来透着与我们有那么一种割不断的血缘关系，这，也许就是此书在美国乃至全球都特别畅销的原因吧！

最后我想申明的是，第一读者身份在我是弥足珍惜的，因为，宝贝儿子出生时，第一眼看见他的是医生，老爸都摊不上第一读者呢！

我眼中的 ……

好书，爱不释手！

★ 读者 王汐子（女，2009年留学美国，攻读大学传媒专业）《小屁孩日记》在美国掀起的阅读风潮可不是盖的，在我留学美国的这一年中，不止一次目睹这套书对太平洋彼岸人民的巨大影响。高速公路上巨大的广告宣传牌就不用说了，我甚至在学校书店买课本时看到了这套书被大大咧咧地摆上书架，"小屁孩"的搞笑日记就这样理直气壮地充当起了美国大学生的课本教材！为什么这套书如此受欢迎？为什么一个普普通通的小男孩能让这么多成年人捧腹大笑？也许可以套用一个万能句式"每个人心中都有一个XXX"。每个人心中都有一个小屁孩，每个人小时候也有过这样的时光，每天都有点鸡毛蒜皮的小烦恼，像作业这么多怎么办啦，要考试了书都没有看怎么办啦……但是大部分时候还是因为调皮捣蛋被妈妈教训……就这样迷迷糊糊地走过了"小屁孩"时光，等长大后和朋友们讨论后才恍然大悟，随即不禁感慨，原来那时候我们都一样呀……是呀，全世界的小屁孩都一样！

★ 读者 zhizhimother（发表于2009-06-12）在杂志上看到这书的介绍，一时冲动在当当上下了单，没想到，一买回来一家人抢着看，笑得前仰后合。我跟女儿一人抢到一本，老公很不满意，他嘟囔着下一本出的时候他要第一个看。看多了面孔雷同的好孩子的书，看到这本，真是深有感触，我们的孩子其实都是这样长大的！

轻松阅读　捧腹大笑

★　这是著名的畅销书作家小巫的儿子Sam口述的英语和中文读后感：我喜欢《小屁孩日记》，因为Greg是跟我们一样的普通孩子。他的故事很好玩儿，令我捧腹大笑，他做的事情很搞笑，有点儿傻乎乎的。书里的插图也很幽默。

★　读者 dearm暖baby（发表于2009-07-29）我12岁了，过生日时妈妈给我买了这样两本书，真的很有趣！一半是中文，一半是英文，彻底打破了"英文看不懂看下面中文"的局限！而且这本书彻底地给我来了次大放松，"重点中学"的压力也一扫而光！总之，两个字：超赞！

孩子爱上写日记了！

★　读者 ddian2003（发表于2009-12-22）正是于丹的那几句话吸引我买下了这套书。自己倒没看，但女儿却用了三天学校的课余时间就看完了，随后她大受启发，连着几天都写了日记。现在这书暂时搁在书柜里，已和女儿约定，等她学了英文后再来看一遍，当然要看书里的英文了。所以这书还是买得物有所值的。毕竟女儿喜欢！！

做个"不听话的好孩子"

★　读者 水真爽（发表于2010-03-27）这套书是买给我上小学二年级的儿子的。有时候他因为到该读书的时间而被要求从网游下来很恼火。尽管带着气，甚至眼泪，可是读起这本书来，总是能被书中小屁孩的种种淘气出格行为和想法弄得哈哈大笑。书中的卡通漫画也非常不错。这种文字漫画形式的日记非常具有趣味性，老少咸宜。对低年级孩子或爱画漫画的孩子尤其有启发作用。更重要的是提醒家长们要好好留意观察这些"不怎么听话"的小屁孩们的内心世界，他们的健康成长需要成人的呵护引导，但千万不要把他们都变成只会"听大人话"的好孩子。

对照《小屁孩日记》分享育儿体验

★　读者 gjrzj2002@＊＊＊.＊＊＊（发表于2010-05-21）看完四册书，我想着自己虽然不可能有三个孩子，但一个孩子的成长经历至今仍记忆犹新。儿子还是幼儿的时候，比较像曼尼，在爸妈眼中少有缺点，真是让人越看越爱，想要什么就基本上能得到什么。整个幼儿期父母对孩子肯定大过否定。上了小学，儿子的境地就不怎么从容了，上学的压力时时处处在影响着他，小家伙要承受各方面的压力，父母、老师、同学，太过我行我素、大而化之都是行不通的，比如没写作业的话，老师、家长的批评和提醒是少不了的，孩子在慢慢学着适应这种生活，烦恼也随之而来，这一阶段比较像格雷，虽然儿子的思维还没那么丰富，快乐和烦恼的花样都没那么多，但处境差不多，表扬和赞美不像以前那样轻易就能得到了。儿子青年时代会是什么样子我还不得而知，也不可想象，那种水到渠成的阶段要靠前面的积累，我希望自己到时候能平心静气，坦然接受，无论儿子成长成什么样子。

气味相投的好伙伴

★　上海市外国语大学附属第一实验中学，中预10班，沈昕仪Elaine：《小屁孩日记》读来十分轻松。虽然没有用十分华丽的语言，却使我感受到了小屁孩那缤纷多彩的生活，给我带来无限的欢乐。那精彩的插图、幽默的文字实在是太有趣了，当中的故事在我们身边都有可能发生，让人身临其境。格雷总能说出我的心里话，他是和我有着共同语言的朋友。所以他们搞的恶作剧一直让我跃跃欲试，也想找一次机会尝试一下。不知道别的读者怎么想，我觉得格雷挺喜欢出风头的。我也是这样的人，总怕别人无视自己。当看到格雷蹦出那些稀奇古怪的点子的时候，我多想帮他一把啊——毕竟我们是"气味相投"的同类人嘛。另一方面，我身处在外语学校，时刻都需要积累英语单词，但这件事总是让我觉得枯燥乏味。而《小屁孩日记》帮了我的大忙：我在享受快乐阅读的同时，还可以对照中英文学到很多常用英语单词。我发现其实生活中还有很多事情值得我们去用笔写下来。即使是小事，这些童年的故事也是很值得我们回忆的。既然还生活在童年，还能够写下那些故事，又何乐而不为呢？

画出我心中的"小屁孩"

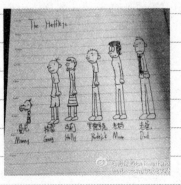

邓博笔下的赫夫利一家

读者@童_Cc.与@曲奇做的"小屁孩"手抄报

亲爱的读者，你看完这本书后，有什么感想吗？请来电或是登录本书的博客与我们分享吧！等本书再版时，这里也许换上了你的读后感呢！

我们的电话号码是：020-83795744；博客地址是：blog.sina.com.cn/wimpykid；微博地址是：weibo.com/wimpywimpy。